From the Pages of Beowulf

Hail! We have heard tales sung of the Spear-Danes,
the glory of their war-kings in days gone by,
how princely nobles performed heroes' deeds!

(PAGE 3, LINES 1–3)

"They knew the power of my strength—
for they had watched when from battles I came,
stained with blood of foes: once I bound five,
destroyed the kin of giants; and in the sea slew
water-monsters at night while in dire distress;
won vengeance for Weders, ground down hateful foes—
those asked for woe. And now with Grendel,
that horrid demon, I shall hold alone
a meeting with the monster."   (PAGES 16–17, LINES 418–426)

Then from the moors that were thick with mist,
Grendel emerged, wrapped in the anger of God.

(PAGE 26, LINES 710–711)

There is no easy way,
to flee from one's fate—try as one may—
but every soul-bearer, every child of men,
each dweller on earth, is destined to seek
his appointed place, compelled by necessity,
with his body held fast in its bed of death,
to sleep after feasting.   (PAGE 35, LINES 1002–1008)

"Have joy of this neck-ring, beloved Beowulf,
with good fortune in youth, and use well this mail-shirt
from our people's treasures, and savor prosperity,

win fame through your skill, and give my sons here
your friendly counsel. I shall remember to give you reward.
For what you did here, men will forever
sing songs of praise, both near and far-off,
even as far as the sea flows round the headlands,
the home of the winds. Be ever blessed while you live,
a noble lord." (PAGE 42, LINES 1216–1225)

"Do not grieve, wise warrior! It is better for each man
that he avenge his friend than to mourn him much."
(PAGE 47, LINES 1384–1385)

Do not foster pride,
glorious warrior! (PAGE 59, LINES 1760–1761)

Then the monster began to spew forth flames,
burning bright dwellings; light from fires shot up,
while the men watched in horror. (PAGE 77, LINES 2312–2314)

"In the time I was given,
I lived in my own land, ruling my people well,
never turning to treachery, or swearing to oaths
contrary to right. In all this I take comfort and joy
when now I am stricken with death-dealing wounds."
(PAGE 90, LINES 2736–2740)

They sang of his valor, and his deeds of great strength,
with all their power praising the hero—as it is fitting
for a man with his words to praise his friendly lord,
share the love from his heart, when the lord must go,
passing beyond the bounds of his body.
(PAGES 104–105, LINES 3173–3177)

BEOWULF

A New Translation
with an Introduction and Notes
by John McNamara

George Stade
Consulting Editorial Director

BARNES & NOBLE CLASSICS
NEW YORK

JB

BARNES & NOBLE CLASSICS
NEW YORK

Published by Barnes & Noble Books
122 Fifth Avenue
New York, NY 10011

www.barnesandnoble.com/classics

Though its author and precise date of composition is unknown—scholars have argued it was written as early as 650 A.D.—the only existing manuscript copy of *Beowulf* dates to 1000.

Originally published in trade paperback format in 2005 by Barnes & Noble Classics with new Translation, Introduction, Notes, Biography, Chronology, Map: *The World of Beowulf*, Note on the Translation, Genealogies, Inspired By, Comments & Questions, and For Further Reading.
This hardcover edition published in 2007.

Introduction, A Note on the Translation, Appendix: Genealogies, Notes, and For Further Reading
Copyright © 2005 by John McNamara.

Translation of Beowulf by John McNamara, Note on the Unknown Author of *Beowulf*,
The World of *Beowulf* and the Anglo-Saxons, Map: *The World of Beowulf*,
Inspired by *Beowulf*, and Comments & Questions,
Copyright © 2005 by Barnes & Noble, Inc.

Beowulf
ISBN-13: 978-1-59308-383-0
ISBN-10: 1-59308-383-1
LC Control Number 2006939768

Produced and published in conjunction with:
Fine Creative Media, Inc.
322 Eighth Avenue
New York, NY 10001

Michael J. Fine, President and Publisher

Printed in the United States of America

QM

3 5 7 9 10 8 6 4 2

The Unknown Author of Beowulf

Around the year 1000, scribes set down a narrative poem about the Scandinavian hero Beowulf. In the alliterative, unrhymed, four-beat meter of Old English poetry, the epic depicts Beowulf's encounters with the marauding monster Grendel and Grendel's mother, and the hero's final battle against a fearful dragon.

It is generally believed that the *Beowulf* manuscript was composed in Anglo-Saxon England using Old English, which was spoken from the early 400s to around 1100. The identity of the poet remains unknown, and what is surmised about the author is historical, genealogical, and linguistic conjecture. The poem was composed following the conversion of England to Christianity, and *Beowulf*'s author and the creators of the manuscript were undoubtedly Christian, but the poem is an amalgam of Christian and pagan values. Significantly, *Beowulf* is among the first vernacular poems in English literature.

Bound up with several other works, *Beowulf* lay dormant in an unknown monastery until 1563, when, after the dissolution of the English monasteries, it emerged into history just long enough for Lawrence Nowell, dean of Litchfield, to inscribe his name on its pages. The manuscript found its way into the library of Sir Robert Cotton (1571–1631), an antiquarian and member of Parliament whose manuscripts, including *Beowulf*, became part of the British Library. In 1731 a fire left the pages of the manuscript singed and powdery. Grímur Jónsson Thorkelin (1752–1829), an Icelandic linguist and archivist working at the University of Copenhagen, made the first transcriptions of the poem. Napoléon's bombardment of the Danish capital in 1807 destroyed Thorkelin's house and the manuscript, but the scholar published the first printed edition of *Beowulf* in 1815.

In the twentieth century, J. R. R. Tolkien (best known for his *The Lord of the Rings* trilogy, which is based on Beowulf) and other scholarly researchers firmly established the historical and literary importance of the epic. Whether approached as a work of great literature or a rousing tale, *Beowulf* continues to fascinate first-time readers and scholars alike.

Table of Contents

The World of Beowulf
and the Anglo-Saxons

55 B.C.E.	Julius Caesar begins leading military expeditions into Britain.
43 C.E.	Emperor Claudius launches a successful Roman invasion of Britain.
122	Romans build Hadrian's Wall, defending the province from invasions by barbarians from the north.
410	Roman legions are withdrawn from Britain.
413	*The City of God*, by Saint Augustine of Hippo, begins to appear.
c.450	Germanic tribes—the Angles, Jutes, and Saxons—begin arriving in Britain and ward off invasions by the Picts and the Scots.
521	Hygelac, king of the Geats, whose story is told in *Beowulf*, is killed in a raid against the Frisians.
597	Pope Gregory sends Saint Augustine to England on a mission to convert Britain to Roman Christianity. Augustine lands at Ebbsfleet and converts King Ethelbert of Kent, the first Christian ruler in England. Augustine remains in England and establishes a holy see at Canterbury; he will be known as Saint Augustine of Canterbury.
627	Northumbrian King Edwin and his counselors accept Christianity. Bishop Paulinus of Kent baptizes the populace.
664	The Synod of Whitby endorses the supremacy of Roman Christianity over Celtic tradition.
731	Bede, the scholar and historian, completes his *History of the English Church and Peoples*.
757	Offa becomes king of Mercia. During his reign, which will end in 796, he consolidates power in Mercia. He builds Offa's Dike, a massive fortification, to defend Britain against invasion from Wales.

814   Charlemagne, emperor of the Holy Roman Empire, dies at Aachen.

866   Vikings (Scandinavian raiders), who have been launching attacks on Britain since the late eighth century, conquer York, and the city becomes the Scandinavian capital in England. Largely consisting of Danes, these Vikings are all simply called "Danes" in prominent English sources.

886   King Alfred the Great (871–899), who has prevented the Danes from overtaking Wessex, and thus all of England, captures London from Viking occupiers. The boundaries of the Danelaw, the "Danish" territories in Britain, are established.

c.892   The *Anglo-Saxon Chronicle*, a history of the Anglo-Saxons, appears.

924   Athelstan, Alfred's grandson, becomes king and will soon proclaim himself ruler of all of England.

c.1000   A manuscript containing the text of *Beowulf* is written. The work is bound together with four other pieces: *The Life of Saint Christopher, The Wonders of the East, Alexander's Letter to Aristotle*, and *Judith*.

1016–   Cnut (Canute) and his sons, Harold Harefoot and Harthacnut
1042   (Hardecanute), reign as Danish kings of England.

1042   The old Wessex line of Alfred the Great is restored as Edward the Confessor becomes king.

1066   On October 14 the Battle of Hastings ends with victory for William the Conqueror, the first Norman king of England, over forces led by the Anglo-Saxon king Harold. During the so-called Norman Conquest that ensues, William brings all of England under Norman rule, often by brutal force.

1536   King Henry VIII of England begins the dissolution of the monasteries.

1563   Lawrence Nowell, dean of Litchfield, inscribes his name on the first page of the *Beowulf* manuscript.

1631   Sir Robert Cotton, an antiquarian and member of Parliament whose library contains the *Beowulf* manuscript, dies.

1700   The Cotton library is bequeathed to the British Library.

1731   Much of the British Library is damaged in a fire, and the only surviving *Beowulf* manuscript is nearly destroyed.

1786   Grímur Jónsson Thorkelin (1752–1829), an Icelandic

archivist and scholar, comes to the British Library searching for documents pertaining to Danish literature and history. He makes two transcriptions of the *Beowulf* manuscript, labeled as a Danish epic, and takes them to Copenhagen.

1807   During the Napoleonic Wars, Copenhagen is bombarded and Thorkelin's house destroyed. His work on the manuscript is lost, and he starts over.

1815   The first printed edition of *Beowulf*, based on Thorkelin's transcriptions and editing, appears.

1936   J. R. R. Tolkien publishes his essay "*Beowulf*: The Monsters and the Critics," one of several twentieth-century scholarly works that establish the epic poem as a masterpiece of English literature.

Introduction

Beowulf is generally regarded as the first true masterpiece in English literature, but generations of readers have also found the epic to be so filled with complexities that its qualities are not always easy to define. The work provides us with a unique representation of the distant world of the early Middle Ages in Northern Europe, and yet in its very complexity it disrupts our commonplace simplifications of that culture and its historical period. We know that the poem was composed in Anglo-Saxon England using Old English, which was spoken from the early 400s to around 1100 (when, after the Norman Conquest of 1066, the language changed to Middle English). We also know that the only manuscript in which *Beowulf* survives can be dated from around the year 1000, having endured the effects of time and even of fire, and its present resting place is the British Library.

Even so, we do not know when the poem was composed, and scholars differ so widely on this point that some would date it in the early 700s, while others would place it in the 900s, or possibly even slightly later. This debate is not a matter of interest only to antiquarians, since the time to which we assign the composition of *Beowulf*, at least in its present form, will affect how we interpret key features of the poem. Moreover, while composed in Old English, this earliest literary masterpiece in our language is set in Scandinavia, and virtually all of the characters are Scandinavian. Why this should be so is still a mystery, especially given the often troubled relations between Anglo-Saxons and Scandinavian Vikings during this period.

Other mysteries likewise abound. We do not know who composed the poem in the form in which it exists in the manuscript. Scholars have generally taken it for granted that the poet was a man, but recent archeological research has unearthed evidence of women serving as scribes in monastic houses. Thus, it is at least possible that a woman could have been involved at some stage of the production of the manuscript. We do know that the poet was working with materials that were, at least in certain notable cases, inherited from a store of traditions. Thus, in addition to the main plot, there are several subplots embedded in the narrative that were drawn from these traditions. As a consequence, many scholars in the nineteenth century believed that *Beowulf* was composed of many separate traditional lays, or sung narratives, but scholars are now generally convinced that a single poet created the poem as we know it, though it was written down by two different scribes. Especially since J. R. R. Tolkien's famous "*Beowulf:* The Monsters and the Critics" was published in 1936 (see For Further Reading), most scholars have stressed the unity of the poem, including its unity of authorship, and have sought to discover the keys to its artistic construction. Even so, there are still fundamental questions about the kind of unity one may find, both in terms of theme and in terms of structure—and even more fundamental questions about the kind of unity one would require in order to judge the success of the poem as a work of art.

Questions about the composition of the epic lead to further questions about the role of the author: How did the poet compose? What kinds of choices did the poet make? On what basis? To what effect? Clearly, all of these questions presuppose an author who made conscious and deliberate artistic choices in selecting, arranging, and highlighting certain characters and actions, while assigning others to subsidiary roles in the narrative. But what if the poet were not an original creator in our modern Romantic and Post-Romantic sense? What if we are dealing here with a traditional poet in the full sense of the term "traditional"? Such a poet would be working with, and to some extent be constrained by, the traditional nature of the narratives circulating in the culture—and retained in the cultural memory in forms that themselves conferred value on the narratives.

Then there is the issue of oral composition. Milman Parry and Albert Lord conducted extremely influential research, first on Homer and then on living Serbo-Croatian poets, showing that singers of traditional tales composed their works orally—and during the very act of performing them. This composing-as-performing was only possible, they argued, because the materials the singers used were largely formulaic. The theory of oral composition will be discussed in greater detail below, but it is important to note here that scholars soon applied it to *Beowulf* (starting in the 1950s), thus raising the questions of what kind of "author" would have composed the

Anglo-Saxon epic and what kind of "composing" that would have been. Debates over these questions have come to dominate much of the criticism of the poem.

Moreover, there is the perplexing mystery about the audience for whom *Beowulf* was intended. While it is commonplace to view literary works from the perspective of their authors, it is not always recognized that audience is a vital force in the creative process. This is especially true for an art that represents traditional stories and values in performances that are shaped, at least in part, by the expectations of the audience. And so we may well ask, who was the audience for *Beowulf*? First of all, was it basically English, or was it Anglo-Scandinavian? The numerous references to historical legends about Scandinavians and their struggles for power with and against one another suggest a collective cultural memory that reaches well beyond England to the far North. These legends frequently appear in the poem as fragments, without coherent chronological order, presupposing an audience that already knew the main outlines of a larger narrative of which the fragmentary allusions were parts—and this audience may have recognized meanings in these bits of legendary history that we can no longer fully trace. After decades of warfare, starting at the end of the eighth century, there were parts of eastern England in which Scandinavians had settled more or less peaceably and where they had largely assimilated Anglo-Saxon culture, especially at times in the 900s. Yet scholars are by no means agreed that *Beowulf* was the product of such an Anglo-Scandinavian community.

Even more perplexing is the question of values and beliefs in the poem. The world of *Beowulf* is the world of heroic epic, with its legendary fights among larger-than-life figures, both human and monstrous, its scenes of feasting in great beer halls presided over by kings, its accounts of bloody feuds trapping men and women alike in cycles of violence, its praise of giving riches to loyal followers rather than amassing wealth for oneself, its moments of magic in stories of powers gained or lost—and over all, a sense of some larger force that shapes their destinies, both individual and collective. Readers have often looked upon this long-gone heroic world for a glimpse of a pagan past in Northern Europe before Christianity was brought by foreign missionaries, yet the poem is filled with references to the new religion and the power of its God. This tension between the ancient past and what was, in the time of the poet, a new world-view disturbed many romantic and nationalistic critics in the nineteenth and early twentieth centuries. They sought in *Beowulf* the origins of Germanic, including Scandinavian, culture—or at least clues from which that culture could be reconstructed. Yet many were for the most part frustrated, for they saw the epic of Northern antiquity "marred" by the intrusions of foreign beliefs and values, such as the Christianity imposed by missionaries from the Mediterranean South, and equally "marred" by the fantastic fights with monsters in the center of the poem, while the historical materials that most interested them were placed on the outer edges. In this view, the poem simply was not the poem that it should have been.

However, the great work of Friedrich Klaeber, and especially the influence of Tolkien, cited above, would change all that. In recent times, scholars have not only stressed the Christian element as integral to the poem as a whole, but they have spent enormous energy in ferreting out its sources and functions. All of which brings us back, not just to the question of the poet, but more importantly to the question of the audience. After all, the poet was composing the work for a community that already shared certain core values, though those values appear at times to emerge from a moment of cultural transition between the memory of the old and the power of the new. So, once again, we are faced with complexity, and attempts to reduce *Beowulf* to some single, or at least predominant, world-view cannot explain the creative tensions in this complexity.

Yet there are further questions about audience. Did it consist, as some scholars have proposed, of people so well versed in Christian teachings, and even in learned theology, that it would have been a monastic community? The answer is by no means clear. We do have the famous letter from Alcuin to the monks of Lindisfarne (797) enjoining them not to include secular heroic narratives in their entertainments. But we also have the even more famous story of the poet Caedmon in Bede's *History of the English Church and People* (731), which shows the members of the monastery at Whitby singing narrative lays, while accompanying themselves on the harp. Their lays must have been secular since it was only after the miracle of Caedmon's poetic inspiration that Christian biblical narratives were set to traditional Anglo-Saxon poetic forms. Such a community would not only house scholars, as well as monks with considerably less education, but also the monastic *familia* was made up of all the lay people—men, women, and children—who occupied and generally worked the lands surrounding (and dependent on) the monastery.

Our modern view of medieval monasteries has been shaped by later reforms, in which walled structures often shut reclusive monks in cloistered protection from the temptations of the larger world. But in Anglo-Saxon England, the monasteries were generally open to the social world, and the *Rule of St. Benedict* lays great stress on the need to extend hospitality to all who come to the community. We also have depictions in monastic works, such as lives of the saints, of storytelling events that included monks and laypeople alike. Thus, even if one were to claim that *Beowulf* was aimed at a monastic audience, it is clear that such an audience would most probably include many who were not monks. And, of course, one need not postulate a monastic audience at all in order to account for the Christian element in the poem. For the dominant ethos of the poem is a celebration of the values of heroic society, and while the poet-narrator's comments often reflect a Christian point of view, the heroic values in the poem are in themselves primarily secular. Or do we have, once again, a complex creative tension between the two?

Thematic Unity of Heroic and Christian Values

As mentioned earlier, during the nineteenth and early twentieth centuries, some scholars regarded *Beowulf* as an essentially pagan epic depicting, and even glorifying, the worldview and practices of prehistoric Northern European culture—the culture that was described in considerable detail by the Roman historian Tacitus in his *Germania* (around the year 98). In this view, Christianity came northward as an alien culture, and as it spread, the earlier cultural materials became overlaid by what was sometimes called the "Christian coloring." In the case of *Beowulf*, this meant that the poem must originally have consisted of heroic lays that at some distant time had been stitched together into something like the epic that has come down to us. But along the way, some "meddling monks" must have been so disturbed by this celebration of a pre-Christian tradition, and so eager to appropriate its power for themselves, that one or more of them added Christian elements, perhaps in the process of writing down the work in manuscript form. Thus, these elements were not only not integral to the poem, but they could be peeled away to see the remains of the nearly lost earlier epic. Such a view represented the poem as thematically inconsistent, if not downright contradictory, in the form given it by the political ambitions of monastic culture. But then, in the early twentieth century, the great scholar Klaeber was in the vanguard of a movement that demonstrated decisively that the Christian elements in the only *Beowulf* we have are so fully integrated into the fabric of the poem that they could not simply have been inserted here and there in the finished work. But what are these elements, and how do they function?

Early in the poem, after Grendel has begun ravaging Hrothgar's hall and gobbling down his men, the Danes sought help from the only supernatural force they knew:

> Many noble Danes
> sat often in council to consider what advice
> was best for the band of strong-hearted warriors
> to defend against sudden attacks of terror.
> For a time they prayed in heathen temples,
> worshipping idols, and pleading with words
> for the Slayer of Souls to come to their aid
> in the nation's crisis. Such then was their custom,
> the hope of heathens; in their hearts
> they bore hell, they knew not the Creator,
> the Judge of all deeds—neither acknowledged the Lord,
> nor knew how to praise the Protector of Heaven,
> the Ruler of Glory. Woe be to the one,
> who through terrible sin, would shove his soul
> into the fire's embrace, foregoing all hope,
> with no chance of change! Happy the one,
> who after his death-day, may seek the Ruler
> for peace and protection in the Father's arms (lines
> 171–188).

The poet-narrator, whoever he may have been, is clearly distancing himself here from the beliefs and practices of the characters in the poem. They were heathens, but he knows the true God. Moreover, he also does not simply observe the difference between their world-view and his own, but he describes their beliefs in the most disparaging terms—praying at altars of idol-worship for help from the Slayer of Souls. Such language was commonplace in monastic writings, as we can see in Bede's great *History* and in numerous saints' lives. But we might not expect the poet-narrator to go on at such length to assure his audience of his Christian beliefs and, at least by implication, to confirm the audience in the same beliefs. Even so, this passage comes right before the introduction of Beowulf, who will become the agent for saving the Danes from the terror of Grendel. The hero, like them, is a "heathen," but he is apparently God's instrument in defeating the monstrous forces of evil.

The poet-narrator has already made it clear that Grendel is one of those forces of evil—"a fiend from hell" (line 101)—and that the struggle to come would be, as in the past, a struggle between God and the dark diabolical Enemy:

> Grendel was the name of this ghastly stranger,
> famed wanderer in wastelands, who held the moors,
> the fens and fastnesses. Once this unhappy beast
> dwelt in the country of monstrous creatures,
> after the Creator had condemned all those
> among Cain's kin—the eternal Lord
> avenged the crime of the one who killed Abel.
> For Cain got no joy from committing that wrong,
> but God banished him far away from mankind.
> From him all wicked offspring were born:
> giants and elves, and evil demon-creatures,
> and gigantic monsters—those who fought God,
> time beyond time. But God repaid them! (lines 102–114).

Thus, Beowulf's coming fight with Grendel is placed within the context of the cosmic combat between God and the Devil, with Beowulf by implication serving as God's champion in the great contest. Later on, in the fight down in the mere against Grendel's mother, this implication is made quite explicit.

Beowulf had defeated Grendel, but Grendel's mother stormed

into Heorot to avenge her son by killing one of the chieftains among the warriors. The feud has been renewed. So Beowulf must now seek vengeance for the beloved Dane. He swims down through the treacherous waters of the mere to her underground lair, and he engages her in the kind of hand-to-hand combat that had been successful against her son. As they wrestle, she manages to exert all her strength, so he slips and falls. She then sits astride his body and attempts to pierce through his ringed-mail shirt with her dagger:

> Then the son of Ecgtheow [Beowulf], stout hero of the
>   Geats,
> would have journeyed to death, under wide earth,
> except that the battle-shirt, the mail made for war,
> provided protection—and the holy God
> decreed which was the victor. For the wise Lord,
> the Ruler of Heaven, decided according to right,
> so the hero of the Geats easily got to his feet (lines
>   1550–1556).

Once again, we not only have a dramatic presentation of action, but also the poet-narrator's commentary on the significance of that action. This happens again and again throughout the epic, so that the back-and-forth movement between action and commentary becomes a kind of dialectic joining the major themes of the heroic warrior culture (in action) and the new perspective of Christian belief (in commentary). This dialectic is so fundamental to the thematic structure of *Beowulf* that it is a major factor in the unity of the whole.

Narrative Structure

As noted earlier, most scholars have followed Tolkien in regarding *Beowulf* as essentially unified, though there has been some disagreement about the nature of this unity, and a few scholars have begun to question the need to claim some form of unity in the work—as if to justify our continuing admiration for the epic. But let us leave aside these debates for the time being and concentrate on what the poem presents us as its narrative structure. For example, it is clear that the main line of the story features the character and actions of

Beowulf himself, yet it is also clear that Beowulf is represented in quite different ways in the early action and in the later stages of the narrative. Taking an overall view, we can see three major episodes in his life as warrior hero: his fights with Grendel, Grendel's mother, and the dragon. Still taking this overall view, we can also see that the life of the hero divides into two parts. First we learn of his youthful exploits in Denmark defending Hrothgar's hall and the people against Grendel and Grendel's mother. Then, after a transitional section explaining how Beowulf came to be king of the Geats, we are told simply that he ruled "for fifty winters" until the terror of the night-flying dragon called him forth to his final battle. Thus, the narrative structure appears as threefold or twofold, depending on which set of features is brought into clearest focus, the fights with the monsters or the stages in the hero's life and career.

At this point, we might simply agree with Tolkien and others that the epic is constructed around a set of oppositions—youth versus age, light versus dark, heroic versus elegiac, and so forth. Here we have the conception of "organic unity" promoted by the famous Romantic poet and theorist, Samuel Taylor Coleridge, who saw such unity in the ways opposing forces in a work may be held in a state of tension balanced against one another. Thus, in *Beowulf* one could see a balancing of symbolic oppositions in the two-part structure of the whole: for example, in the representation of the young, vigorous, self-confident hero fighting Grendel and Grendel's mother as poised in a kind of dialectical relationship with the later depiction of Beowulf as old, no longer able to fight without weapons, somewhat doubtful of his prowess, and fatally wounded by the dragon's fangs. Or, perhaps one might see this unity-in-opposition in the depictions of Beowulf first as hero and loyal follower, and then later as a king responsible for the protection and welfare of his people.

In this view, there is ultimately a tragic irony in the hero becoming king and still trying to act out the role of heroic warrior, which leads not only to his own fall but that of his people as well, as predicted by Wiglaf, the Messenger, and the woman mourner at the end of the epic. Here, too, we have an overall unity of the twofold structure in which neither part by itself could produce this tragic irony. But do such interpretations really solve the questions of unity in the narrative? Up to this point, the argument for unity has focused on the character of the hero. Clearly, the great fights that engage most of our interest in the poem are related to one another through unity of character. But what happens if we shift our focus to the numerous actions that constitute the plotting of the narrative?

When we descend from the heights from which we might see *Beowulf* as a whole, we find ourselves in a narrative that does not simply move in a straight line, but that moves forward and backward, with various side trips into stories that sometimes involve Beowulf and sometimes do not. Here we are confronted with another kind of question about unity. Do we work to reconcile the seeming "digressions" with the main plot, thereby defending the narrative against charges of disunity, or do we simply accept the very looseness of the structure as the inevitable consequence of its being the kind of work it is, and produced according to aesthetic norms very different from those promoted by, say, Aristotle?

The case for the defense of unity has typically rested on essentially Aristotelian grounds. In his *Poetics*, Aristotle presents his own famous conception of "organic unity," a biological metaphor in which all parts must serve functions integrally related to one another and therefore to the whole. Moreover, Aristotle claims that what makes "poetry more philosophical than history" is that history presents events as they occurred in temporal order, whereas poetry seeks, or should seek, for the often underlying causal connections among events, whether these events actually occurred or not. But he does not leave matters there. Aristotle provides two tests for "organic unity": If a part of a narrative can be either placed in another position, or even removed altogether, without disrupting the plot, then the plot is not truly organically unified. Yet it is only fair to add that Aristotle appears to have allowed for degrees of unity in plot construction. His ideal model was *Oedipus the King*, and when he spoke of Homer, he found the epic to be less tightly unified—and presumably less esthetically satisfying—than his favorite play. Now, if we apply these norms to *Beowulf*, as many have done, we encounter a whole set of problems rather different from those described above in the twofold or threefold structural models. But these problems will only become evident by analyzing some specific passages in detail.

Let us begin with the beginning. The narrative does not begin with Beowulf, or even in his homeland of the Geats, but rather with a genealogy of Danish kings. The poet-narrator reminds his audience that they have heard tales told about the Spear-Danes (one of several epithets applied to them), and he proceeds to describe the power that King Scyld, founder of the royal line, exercised over his own people and over neighboring peoples as well, leading up to the observation, "That was a good king!" We then enter the borderline between myth and legendary history as we learn of the mysterious coming of Scyld to his people as a child, followed by his kingship and his fathering a successor, before dying and being given a spectacular funeral in his ship, which is then cast adrift on the tide to take him on his last journey. His son is Beow, who in turn fathers the father of Hrothgar, who is the Danish king at the time of the poem. Only then do we hear of the building of Hrothgar's great hall, Heorot, which is the site for the bloody man-eating raids by the monster Grendel. Oral reports of these raids reach Beowulf across the sea in Geatland (apparently in southern Sweden), whose journey to aid Hrothgar against Grendel begins the main plot of the work.

The prologue might seem to be rather lengthy to a modern reader, but in the world of *Beowulf* people are always concerned about origins, and even the principal characters are often referred to by their father's names. Such origins would appear to define a person's nature and quality, and thus to dispense with them would be unthinkable. So it is not hard to see how this culture would regard the Danish genealogy as integral to the narrative. Moreover, the epic concludes with another funeral by the sea, when Beowulf is cremated and his barrow is raised as a monument, so there is a symmetry in the plot beginning and ending with funerals.

A somewhat different case is the function of the story of Sigemund, especially as it is immediately followed by the story of Heremod. The tale of the legendary Germanic hero Sigemund is sung by Hrothgar's scop, a teller of traditional tales, during the high-spirited celebration after Beowulf 's victory over Grendel. In the scop's version, Sigemund's early career had already established his fame as a warrior, but then came his greatest achievement:

> . . . the battle-bold hero defeated the dragon,
> the guard of a hoard. Under gray rocks
> this son of a chieftain took his chances alone,

a daring deed—nor was Fitela then with him.
Yet to him it was given to stab with his sword
through the wondrous dragon, clear into the wall,
where the iron stuck. Thus was the dragon slain.
The warrior won the prize by his boldness,
so he now could enjoy the hoard of treasures,
however he wished. The son of Waels [Sigemund]
then loaded the sea-boat, bore to the ship's bosom
the shining wealth—while the dragon melted in flames
    (lines 886–897).

The connection of this tale of monster-slaying with the main plot is obvious: It implicitly compares Beowulf, who has just killed the monster Grendel, with the mythical hero Sigemund, thus serving as a kind of indirect praise poem to honor Beowulf. In addition, this tale anticipates Beowulf's own fight with the dragon at the conclusion of the epic, though, unlike Sigemund, he ends that fight as a tragic hero. Thus, we may conclude that the tale of Sigemund is not a "digression" at all.

    Then, after three lines continuing the praise of Sigemund, the narrative rather abruptly changes course, asserting that this mythic hero outshone Heremod in noble deeds. It seems from other references in the poem that Heremod was a Danish king who preceded the Scyld described at the beginning. Heremod is presented here as a negative model of kingship, the source of much suffering among his people until he was betrayed and assassinated while among the Jutes. Then a connection is made, though a negative one, with Beowulf:

In contrast to him,
Beowulf became to the Danes and all mankind
a far greater friend—while Heremod waded in evil
    (lines 913–915).

Then the narrative returns to a description of the Danes who are celebrating Beowulf's victory. There are several points here that require explanation. First, if the implied comparison of Beowulf with Sigemund functions to praise Beowulf, so also does the contrast between

Heremod and Beowulf function to praise Beowulf. And since both heroes are presented in contrast to the antihero, they are once again, at least by implication, compared with each other in nobility. Second, who is doing the praising or condemning here? The scop is not quoted directly; we only hear him through the voice of the poet-narrator:

> And so he began
> to sing with skill of Beowulf's adventure
> and with masterful talent to perform his tale,
> in words well-woven. He related all things
> he had ever heard told of the legendary deeds
> of Sigemund—many stories till now unsung (lines
>   871–876).

Yet the poet-narrator does not claim that the scop compared Beowulf with Sigemund, though the implication is certainly there. We also do not know when the scop ends his song, and therefore we do not know whether the contrasts of Sigemund and Beowulf with Heremod are made by the scop or by the poet-narrator of the poem as a whole. Even so, the voice we do hear is that of the poet-narrator, and it appears that it is he who makes the comparisons and contrasts. Otherwise, why not simply quote the scop?

We may further note that the logic here is not the logic of Aristotle. The connections are neither causal nor even temporal, but they do follow the logic of association, and this logic is a typical strategy throughout the epic, taking various forms. The poet-narrator begins a story, which by a process of association reminds him of another story, and so he appears to "digress." But the point is that he returns to the original story, which now provides a frame or context in which the associated story has meaning. At the same time, what may at first seem to be a digression turns out to give new meaning to the story into which it is inserted. This pattern can be found throughout *Beowulf,* and it provides further evidence of the artistic complexity of the work. At the same time, we may recognize in this pattern a narrative strategy that is common in oral storytelling—a point to which we shall return in the discussion of oral composition.

In the meantime, it is also important to note that metaphors

other than organic unity have proved fruitful in the quest to understand the structure of this kind of narrative. The medievalist John
Leyerle has proposed an analogy with the intricate interlace patterns
of Anglo-Saxon visual arts, which survive in manuscript illumina-
tions and sculptures, though they may be found in other Northern
art, from Ireland to Scandinavia. It seems plausible that both the
verbal and visual arts would exhibit similar patterns, deriving from a
common cultural imagination. But it is also critical that we bear in
mind that the argument for interlacing in *Beowulf* is based on a metaphor that has its own limitations. For while the eye may travel through
the intricate paths of a picture, it can also see the design all at once, as
a whole. The same is not quite true of verbal arts, since they can only
be experienced in some temporal sequence, and the effort to see a
poem as a whole is an abstraction quite different from seeing a picture
as a whole. Even so, the metaphor continues to provide fascinating
suggestions about Anglo-Saxon poetry and the other arts.

Another metaphor is that of ring-patterns in the narrative, which
has been quite fully developed by John D. Niles and others. There are
numerous repetitions in *Beowulf*, and often one account or reference to an event appears to circle back to an earlier account or reference to the same event. For example, there are several points at
which Beowulf's fight with Grendel is recounted, sometimes at
length and sometimes in brief allusion. If we look at the narrative in
linear terms, these recountings seem to be mere "repetitions" and
therefore further evidence of the looseness of plotting in the work as
a whole. But if we look at such patterns as rings in which the narrative circles back on itself in such instances, then it would appear that
we have come rather closer to grasping the compositional principles
that the poet-narrator is employing. Beyond that, once we recognize
such ring patterns, we also begin to see that there are rings within
rings, or even rings within rings within rings, in complex relations
to one another. The figure of the ring is attractive in part because of
the prevalence of literal rings and ring-giving throughout the story,
but also because it provides an insight into the artfulness of the kind
of narration that we find in *Beowulf*. Once again, we must face the
fact that the epic does not always conform to the expectations of at
least some modern readers. It was composed in another cultural
milieu, according to artistic traditions different from ours, yet there

are great rewards for us in discovering and appreciating this very "otherness" of the poem—as understood on its own terms.

Poetic Forms

Just as *Beowulf* employs narrative forms expressive of Anglo-Saxon culture, so also will we find poetic forms here that are characteristic of almost all poetry in Old English, but which are rare in poems written since that time. First of all, the poetic line typically consists of two verses, or half-lines, marked by a caesura, or pause, and linked by alliteration. Consider the following example: When Beowulf gives one of his many speeches, it is generally introduced with the line,

> Then Beowulf spoke, the son of Ecgtheow.

Setting aside for the moment the formulaic nature of the line, we may note here that the line actually consists of two half-lines, or verses, separated by a caesural pause. For that reason, most editors of the original Old English put a blank space between the two verses:

> Beowulf mathelode bearn Ecgtheowes.

Also, the sound of the "b" in the first verse is repeated, as alliteration, in the second verse (though not in the translation given above, where "s" is used). This pattern of alliteration thus joins the two verses, or half-lines, into a whole line. (In this system, vowels can alliterate as well as consonants.) Moreover, the verses and whole lines do not follow the kinds of meter we are accustomed to in later poetry—for example, in that of Chaucer, Shakespeare, and many others. They employ instead stress patterns, with alliterating syllables typically receiving strong stresses, and also marking the most important points in the meaning of the line: here, that Beowulf is identified as a son. As long ago as 1885, the great scholar Eduard Sievers described the various patterns of stressed and unstressed syllables in this poetry, and despite several attempts to provide new models, the patterns worked out by Sievers are still fundamental for any study of Old English versification.

Less technical, but also more apparent to most readers, are the kinds of poetic figures commonly used in the poem. The figure that is perhaps most characteristic of this poetry is the kenning. A kenning is typically a compound of two nouns, with the qualities of each now united to create a new metaphor. Examples include "whale's road" or "swan's road" for the sea, "heath-stepper" for a stag, "battle-flasher" for a sword, and "sea-garment" for the sail "worn" by a ship. On the other hand, something like "blade-biter," though certainly a poetic figure, would not be a kenning, since the blade is literally the part of the sword that makes it a sword in the first place. Kennings abound in *Beowulf* and throughout Old English poetry, making creative use of one of the resources of Germanic languages, the almost endless possibilities for joining words in compounds. Some are traditional and formulaic, though others seem more puzzling, perhaps as a sign of the Northern people's love for puzzles as a form of entertainment.

Litotes is another figure that Old English shares with other Northern literatures. The characteristic quality of litotes is understatement, generally ironic and sometimes even humorous, using negatives or double-negatives. We may hear in one case that a warrior is "unready for fighting" when we know that he is actually sleeping, or that a monster is "not unused to ravaging the people." Readers of Old Icelandic sagas will recognize such instances of understatement as a common feature in the Northern imagination. Yet even more pervasive is the use of metonymy. While a metaphor designates something that literally does not exist, a metonym works by association, so that an object can be linked to another object or person and comes to stand for that other object or person. Thus, a king can be "the shield of the people," and we will recognize that what is being designated is the king, even if he is not mentioned in so many words. Throughout *Beowulf*, warriors are associated in this way with weapons, rulers with the gifts they give loyal followers, and monsters with such lairs as the mere or the hoard. Indeed, metonymy is so pervasive that it is tempting to extend the usual sense of the poetic figure to a principle of composition, as in the larger and smaller narrative structures we looked at in the previous section.

The last feature of style that we shall explore here is rooted in the grammatical structures of the poem, what linguists usually call parataxis (literally, placing one thing alongside another) or what is called coordination (versus subordination) in traditional grammar classes. Parataxis entails a series of parallel constructions strung together, one after another, by the use of a coordinating conjunction such as "and." Thus, what we hear is a series of actions—"Beowulf did X, and then Beowulf did Y, and then Beowulf did Z"—without making one action subordinate to another, as "When Beowulf did X, he was forced to do Y, because he had already done Z." (Such subordination is technically called hypotaxis, which literally means placing one thing under another or making it dependent on another.) Closely related to the parallelism in a series of statements is the use of one or more appositives, which provide further information about the person or object or event presented first in a statement. Thus, to use an earlier example, we may see in "Then Beowulf spoke, the son of Ecgtheow" that the second part of the statement provides, in what grammarians call an appositive, further information about the person introduced in the first part. But enough of the grammar lesson. We may well ask what this all has to do with the poetic style of *Beowulf.*

The answer lies in the maneuver usually called variation. Even the most casual reader will recognize the following pattern as occurring throughout the poem:

> The sea-vessel plunged on,
> its neck spraying foam, floating over the flood,
> the tightly bound prow pitching over the streams—
> till the sailors could see the high cliffs of the Geats,
> the well-known headlands, and the ship shot forward,
> buffeted by winds, to land up on the beach (lines
> 1908–1913).

A more prosaic account might simply have said that Beowulf and his men sailed in their ship from Denmark home to Geatland. But what would be lost, of course, would be the poetry, and poetry of a very special kind. After the initial half-line, the next two lines give variations on what was first described. In one sense, those two lines could be struck out, leaving us with

> The sea-vessel plunged on,
> till the sailors could see the high cliffs of the Geats,

which would make perfect sense and would make the description appear more economical. But that is not the economy of Old English poetry. The poet-narrator, and presumably his audience as well, relished the device of variation used here. It is not enough to present the ship in motion, but that motion is enriched by the image of the spray from the neck of the boat cutting through the waves, with that neck suggesting the figure of a beast often seen on the prows of Viking ships, plus a reminder that they are traversing a mighty deep, plus a further description of the way the neck image is produced by the binding of boards together, plus the pitching of the boat in the sea.

Note also how the seamen, as they near their homeland, see "the high cliffs of the Geats" as "the well-known headland." As with metonymy, this parallelism involves a process of association, with one image suggesting another that becomes associated with it. There are so many instances of this kind of variation in *Beowulf* that to quote further examples would almost involve quoting the entire poem.

Oral Composition

Since the 1950s, much attention has been paid to the question of oral composition in *Beowulf*. In order to understand that question, we may turn to the theory developed first by Milman Parry and carried on by his student and colleague in research, Albert B. Lord. Parry was a classical scholar who became interested in the fact that Homer's epics are filled with epithets and other expressions that seemed to him to be formulaic. Athena is frequently introduced as "gray-eyed Athena," Achilles as "swift-footed Achilles," and so on with other characters. Parry suggested that the epic poet using such formulas did not have to invent the description of, say, Athena each time she was introduced because there was already in the tradition a made-up phrasing for this purpose. He cited numerous such cases in Homer and concluded that these formulas were essential functions of traditional oral poetry.

Parry and Lord gradually formulated a hypothesis that poets working in oral tradition, without written texts, would create their narratives, even very long narratives, in the very act of performing before an audience. Such "singers of tales" would not have to memorize their narratives word for word, which in most cases would be virtually impossible, but rather would have been trained by accomplished oral poets in the traditional plots and formulaic expressions for describing people, buildings, gods, weapons, and the like. In order to test this hypothesis, Parry and Lord sought out traditional oral poets, whose art had been passed down into modern times. They found such poets among Serbo-Croatian singers, and their research among these singers confirmed their earlier findings and allowed them to extend and refine their theory of oral composition-in-performance.

In 1953 Francis P. Magoun published a famous study of oral-formulaic poetry in Anglo-Saxon England that quickly drew other scholars to apply the theory to *Beowulf* in detailed analyses. Immediately, a controversy erupted. The main issue appeared to be the question of originality and artistry on the part of the *Beowulf* poet. If the poem consisted largely of traditional formulas, then what kind of originality or artistic mastery did the poet exercise in its creation? Or, what could "creation" even mean in such a case? And if the work of artistic creation in *Beowulf* were so substantially reduced, what would happen to claims that it was a literary masterpiece? These questions were especially crucial to those who adhered to Romantic and Post-Romantic conceptions of the poet as an individual genius creating works of art that were nothing if not original. But gradually the initial passion of the debate subsided as the very definition of "formula" proved less and less clear, and both proponents of oral theory and proponents of the masterful artistry of the poem sought some middle ground. For clearly there is evidence here both of traditional oral poetry and of a very high level of artistry working within traditional forms. Let us look at some of that evidence.

First of all, there are formulaic expressions in many places in *Beowulf*. As we saw earlier, a speech by the hero is generally introduced by the expression,

Then Beowulf spoke, the son of Ecgtheow.

But the same expression can be used to introduce other speakers:

Then Hrothgar spoke, the son of Healfdene.

Then Hygelac spoke, the son of Hrethel.

Then Wiglaf spoke, the son of Weohstan.

And so on. Such expressions unmistakably follow a formula for introducing speakers, and the poet-singer-narrator needs only to insert the proper names for the speaker and for his father into the slots that are already there for that function.

Yet there is no denying the artistic skill with which style and structure are developed, even working with traditional phrasing—as in the example of variation in the description of the Geats sailing home (see above). While we do not know who the poet was or how he composed his poetry, it seems from such evidence that he was thoroughly familiar with traditional forms that were no doubt still being used in oral performances by "singers of tales" in his own time. He also showed an artistic subtlety that we usually associate with writing. Likewise, the audience was probably made up of both literate and nonliterate Anglo-Saxons, and, of course, there may have been several different audiences for the same poem, or even different performances that were shaped by the makeup of different audiences. For example, such a skillful poet would surely have made adjustments in performing the poem for, say, a monastic audience as distinguished from a more secular court audience—or for audiences that mixed individuals of different backgrounds, classes, or education.

While the *Beowulf* poet-singer-narrator may have given oral performances, he may also have committed the epic to writing or performed it for some scribe who did. Such a written version would contain forms designed for oral performance, and this version could have passed through several hands before being copied by the scribes of the surviving manuscript. But we really do not have clear evidence to solve this perplexing problem. So, we may ask, what difference does it make to us as modern readers whether we see features of orality in the poem or not? The point here is that there are some elements of the poem that can be more readily explained if we see them as part of, or at least derived from, oral tradition.

Consider the references to various traditions that are evoked as parts of the cultural memory of both poet and audience. We have already looked at some of these, including references to the near-mythical Sigemund and the references to Christian religion. Let us now consider the numerous references to the Swedish-Geatish wars that occupy much space in the latter part of the poem. These references should not be considered historical in the modern sense of the term. Rather, they are presented in the epic as recollections of historical events. In other words, it appears to have been important for the culture that produced *Beowulf* to maintain these legends in its cultural memory. For out of these legends, as well as others in the poem, this culture constructed its identity—its imagined origins, with the representation of a Heroic Age in which great warriors and their lords fought extraordinary battles against one another, and against monstrous foes and the forces of darkness, only to fall themselves after their moment of glory. Seen in this light, the legends of the Swedish-Geatish wars are by no means the "facts" of history, but they do present facts about the cultural memory and imagination of the poet and audience of *Beowulf*.

In order to see the relevance of oral theory for the ways these legends are used in the epic, we must now turn to the question of their constructions as narratives. The first thing we may note about them is their seeming lack of coherent development, and that may be accounted for by assuming that they derive from some larger traditional narrative in which they do have coherence. Orally developed plots may follow a main narrative line, while constantly interrupting that line with allusions to, or fragments from, other narratives that seem, to the teller and audience alike, related to the main line and to one another. In other words, these allusions to, and fragments of, "other" narratives outside the main plot are, by tradition, taken to be related to the main narrative line. Even so, they are also parts of independent narratives that could be told independently of the "main" plot in which they are currently embedded or to which they are currently attached.

For example, the "singer of tales" could relate the story of Sigemund by itself and, presumably, in its entirety. Yet since such narratives in *Beowulf* generally appear in allusive, fragmentary, elliptical, recursive, nonsequential forms characteristic of scattered recollections, they presuppose a narrative already known, more or less, by the teller and audience. And while that larger narrative may never be fully related in a given context, it remains a necessary condition enabling the teller and audience to see coherence where there would otherwise seem to be only bewildering bits and pieces. We may appreciate the necessity of that condition when we consider how difficult it is for us to comprehend these allusive and fragmentary narrative bits, even with scholarly apparatus and time for reflection, and then consider how much more a listening audience would require at least some prior knowledge of the larger narratives of which these bits are parts.

But enough of theoretical abstraction. Let us now turn to *Beowulf* and analyze a typical set of such narrative bits, which are set in the main plot of the poem, yet presuppose a coherent narrative of their own for full comprehension. The narrative of Geatish-Swedish relations appears in eight allusions or fragments spread throughout the last third (or so) of the poem. In order to demonstrate the problem for interpretation, we may first consider these eight in the narrative order of the poem and then reconstruct them in a chronological sequence.

1. When Beowulf went to report to Hygelac on his Danish expedition, the Geatish king was described with the epithet "the slayer of Ongentheow" (line 1968), an old king of the Swedes. (However, as we learn later, Hygelac did not actually kill him, though he led the attack in which Eofer, one of his warriors, killed Ongentheow.)

2. After Hygelac's death, his son King Heardred was killed by invading Swedes, thus bringing Beowulf to the throne (lines 2200–2210).

3. After Hygelac's death, Queen Hygd offered the throne to Beowulf, who deferred to Heardred. Heardred supported Eanmund and Eadgils, sons of Ohtere, in their feud against their uncle Onela, the Swedish king. The Swedes attacked and killed Heardred, whereupon Beowulf became king and subsequently supported Eadgils' retaliatory attack in which Eadgils appears most likely to have killed Onela and then to have become Swedish king (lines 2369–2396).

4. Beowulf's recollection of Haethcyn killing Herebeald, his older brother, in an archery accident (lines 2435–2443).

5. Beowulf's recollection that when Hrethel died, Haethcyn succeeded him and was attacked by Ohtere and Onela, the sons of the old Swedish king, Ongentheow. When Haethcyn retaliated, he was killed, but he was avenged when Eofor, a warrior under Hygelac's command, killed Ongentheow (lines 2472–2489).

6. Seeing Beowulf suffering alone in the Dragon fight, Wiglaf seized the sword of his father Weohstan (apparently a Swede), which had belonged to Eanmund when Weohstan slew him. Weohstan won Eanmund's sword and war gear in his service to Onela, the Swedish king, who remained silent about the killing of Eanmund, his nephew as well as his enemy. Weohstan later gave the sword and other war gear to his son Wiglaf while then among the Geats (lines 2610–2625).

7. After Beowulf's death, Wiglaf forecast the Geats' total loss because of their shameful flight from their lord in need, making them vulnerable to their enemies (lines 2884–2891).

8. Sent by Wiglaf to the other Geats, the Messenger then forecast doom from Franks and Frisians to the south for Hygelac's earlier raid in Frisia (where Hygelac was killed), as well as from Swedes to the north for the Ravenswood battle where Ongentheow killed Haethcyn and pursued the Geats until Hygelac saved them with a relief force; whereupon Ongentheow retreated to his fortification, was pursued, struck down the Geatish warrior Wulf, whose brother Eofor then killed Ongentheow. Hygelac richly rewarded both brothers, but gave Eofor the greater gift of his only daughter in marriage. The Messenger predicts, in greater detail than Wiglaf, the coming fall of the Geats for Ongentheow's (unavenged) death (lines 2900–3027).

There is, of course, much here that is very confusing to a modern reader, but this is the order in which *Beowulf* presents the narrative of the Swedish-Geatish wars. As the summary shows, each piece of the narrative is a fragment of some larger story, and we are never given that larger story within the epic as it stands. Moreover, these fragmentary references are generally separated by considerable lengths from one another, and they are not presented in chronological order. If we want to make clear their chronological order, we would have to rearrange the eight fragments as follows: The sequence would begin with fragments 4, 5, and 8 (which also partially explains the sense of fragment 1), and then proceed with fragments 2 and 3 together with some details explained by fragment 6, followed by fragment 7 and the last part of fragment 8. (Readers who do not wish to try this exercise will find full explanations of the action of the poem in the notes to the main text.)

If the audience were listening to an oral performance, its members would have to rearrange this sequence in their heads, which would only seem possible if the poet and audience already had a larger traditional narrative in their cultural memory that put all the fragments in meaningful order. Thus, the poet-narrator can "recollect" events from that legendary history to insert in the main plot, whenever allusions to them seem appropriate to him—generally, by the process of association characteristic of oral composition that we considered earlier. It would not be very helpful to postulate instead an audience of readers, since these readers would have the same problem. Unless they were scholars with the professional interest in carrying out the sort of analysis given here, which is extremely unlikely for a secular epic such as this, these readers would also have to have access to the same kind of cultural memory that a listening audience would need. Even if *Beowulf* were presented in a monastic refectory, it would have been read aloud or otherwise performed for the audience, and that audience could not follow large parts of the narrative if they heard them in this epic for the first time. Still, there certainly are learned references in the poem and, especially in the case of religious references, these imply familiarity with textual traditions. And so, when all things are considered, there does seem good reason to see *Beowulf* occupying a borderland somewhere between oral tradition and the world of the book—probably at some time when both lived side-by-side.

Finally, we hear a second side to oral composition in *Beowulf*, as we are constantly reminded that the narrative is fundamentally *aural*. Again and again, the poet-singer uses some variation of the formula, "I have heard," or "I have heard it told," or "I have heard the tale sung." In other words, this is a culture in which what is said must first of all have been heard. And so, in such a culture there is less a boundary between "author" and "audience," than there is a threshold over which hearers of tales may pass to become tellers, and tellers are worth hearing to the extent that they themselves have become creative hearers. And so, while we may never know exactly how *Beowulf* was composed, we can see—or rather hear—in this dialectic of the *oral* and the *aural* yet another manifestation of the artistic complexity of our earliest epic in the English language.

———————————

John McNamara is Professor of English at the University of Houston, where he teaches the early languages and literatures of England, Scotland, and Ireland, with a special focus on their oral traditions. He has published numerous articles in those areas, and with Carl Lindahl and John Lindow he co-edited *Medieval Folklore: An Encyclopedia of Myths, Legends, Tales, Beliefs, and Customs*, 2 vols. (Santa Barbara: ABC–CLIO, 2000), which is now in a revised edition published by Oxford University Press (2002). He has twice won the University of Houston Teaching Excellence Award, and he has also been designated Master Teacher by his college. He lives in the Houston area with his wife Cynthia Marshall McNamara, a specialist in rhetoric and modern British literature, surrounded by their large family.

Acknowledgments

I owe my first and greatest debt to my students in graduate seminars in Old English Language and Literature, and especially in the seminar on *Beowulf* and the Art of Translation. Their insightful questions have made them my teachers, and I have learned much from them. I am also grateful to my table companions in our Old English/Old Icelandic Reading Group, especially Laurel Lacroix, Hilary Mackie, Cynthia Green, and Michael Skupin. In my efforts to catch something of the poetic quality of *Beowulf* I have had the wise counsel of poets Robert Phillips and James Cleghorn, whose suggestions about tone and audience have been invaluable. Hovering over all has been the presence of my late friend and fellow scholar Jeanette Morgan.

I wish to thank George Stade, consulting editorial director for the Barnes & Noble Classics, for inviting me to undertake this project. I am especially grateful to Jeffrey Broesche, general editor for this series, for his constant attention and his unstinting encouragement.

Finally, it gives me great pleasure to acknowledge the tremendous debt I owe to my friend and colleague Carl Lindahl and, of course, to my wife and colleague Cynthia, who has made all possible.

A Note on the Translation

The translation for this edition is based on the authoritative text produced by Friedrich Klaeber, which has been the standard text for citation by scholars for decades, but other editions have been consulted as well. In recent years, there has been a great deal of attention paid to the problems with reading the manuscript, some of which are paleographical—establishing what certain characters and words actually are—and some come from damage to the manuscript. The unique manuscript, dating from around the year 1000, was partially burned in a fire, and other forms of deterioration have occurred through age and the ways the manuscript has been handled. Some of the characters, words, and even whole verses have been reconstructed with the use of various technologies, the most recent being the digitizing of the manuscript for the British Library under the direction of Kevin Kiernan. Even so, if we turn pages in Klaeber's or other modern editions, we will be struck by the number of cases in which editors have enclosed their emendations in square brackets. Most of these are single letters, but in a few cases whole lines have been reconstructed according to the best surmises of modern scholars, based on either linguistic or poetic considerations. Therefore, any translator must consult not only the Klaeber text, but also the work of Kiernan, Bruce Mitchell, Fred C. Robinson, and perhaps others. Since I have also used the excellent student edition of George Jack in courses for graduate students in the early stages of learning Old English, I have also benefited from his work as well. Important work on the text of *Beowulf* continues, as in the research of R. D. Fulk.

The translation given here has several objectives. First of all, it is a poetic translation that attempts to convey at least something of the flavor of the Old English poetry. But as is well known, translating poetry into poetry often faces difficulties in representing the literal sense of the original, and it is a commonplace of translators that one can represent the literal meaning more closely in prose translation. But then much of the poetry of the original is lost. A more seductive problem is the temptation for the translator to draw attention to her or his own poetry—and therefore skill as a poet—at the expense of the original poetry. This is perhaps especially tempting in dramatic scenes of action, though the translator may wish to "enliven" some of the more prosaic passages as well. Another question has been getting increasing attention among translators and theorists of translation: whether producing smoothness and easy accessibility in translating really is superior to representing something of the antiquity and "otherness" of the original. Is it possible that a translation of an old poem might be so successful as modern poetry that the very "otherness" of the original is obscured or even lost? And is it not the very "otherness" of the original that attracted many modern readers in the first place? These questions have been raised mainly in debates about the politics of language and of translation in colonial and postcolonial cultures (for example, Ireland, South Asia, and the Middle East), but such questions can also be raised about our translations of early cultures into our own. In the translation of *Beowulf* given here, every effort has been made to make the poem accessible to modern readers, while at the same time preserving some sense of its "otherness" in diction, syntax, poetic movement, and cultural worldview.

At the same time, it is of course essential to make the often puzzling passages in *Beowulf* clear to readers who are not specialists in Old English. Accordingly, this edition keeps the lines of the translation as close as possible to the positions of the lines in the original, while recognizing that sometimes small rearrangements of verses may be necessary for the sake of clarity. This is especially important in instances of variation, where the sequence of verses follows rules of Old English grammatical usage but obscures the grammatical relations in Modern English. We face a similar problem with pronoun references. These are frequently vague or uncertain in the original, and only careful analysis can make them clear. It may be that non-verbal cues would have designated pronoun references in oral performance (gestures, changes in bodily position, intonation), but these would obviously not work for us. So, in this translation, the actual names of persons and places are used to replace unclear pronouns (Hygelac for "he," Geatland for "it," and the like).

Finally, of course, it is crucial to represent at least something of the vitality of the poetics. As discussed earlier, the poetic line consists of two verses or half-lines, which are separated by a pause and joined by alliteration, typically on strongly stressed syllables. In this translation, almost all of the lines contain some alliteration, though often it has not been possible to reproduce the exact pattern of the original and at the same time convey its sense. In addition, occasionally verses or whole lines are "filled out" to produce metrical regularity. Sometimes the Old English compresses its meaning into wording that, when translated literally into Modern English, would reduce a whole line to a half-line. In a few cases, therefore, the translation expands a word to a phrase—with the provision that the expansion be consistent with poetic usage elsewhere in the epic and that it not alter the fundamental meaning of the line in question. Once again, the value of the translation is to be seen in its loyalty to the original—as a faithful retainer should be to whom the lord has given a great gift.

—John McNamara

The World of Beowulf

Arctic Circle

North Sea

Heatho-Raemas

Swedes

Baltic Sea

Geats

Jutes

Danes

Frisians

Elbe River

Franks

GENEALOGIES

DANES *Scyldings*

Scyld
|
Beow
|
Healfdene

Heorogar — Hrothgar m. Wealhtheow — Halga — Daughter m. Onela

Hrethric — Hrothmund — Freawaru m. Ingeld

Hrothulf

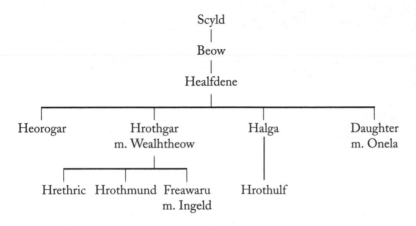

GEATS

Hrethel

Herebeald — Haethcyn — Daughter m. Ecgtheow — Hygelac m. Hygd

Beowulf

Daughter m. Eofer — Heardred

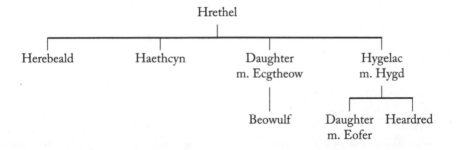

SWEDES *Scylfings*

Ongentheow

Ohtere — Onele m. Hrothgar's sister

Eanmund — Eadgils

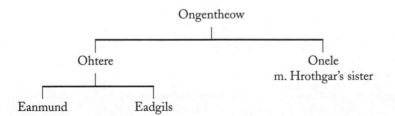

BEOWULF

Prologue

Hail! We have heard tales sung of the Spear-Danes,[1]
the glory of their war-kings in days gone by,
how princely nobles performed heroes' deeds!
    Oft Scyld Scefing* captured the mead halls
from many peoples, from troops of enemies,   5
terrifying their chieftains. Though he was first
a poor foundling, he lived to find comfort;
under heavens he flourished, with honors fulfilled—
till each neighboring nation, those over the whale-road,
bowed under his rule, paid the price of tribute.   10
That was a good king![2]
And then to the king a boy was born,
a son in the hall, who was sent by God
as relief to the Danes; for their ruler well knew
the distress of his people while long without leader   15
before his coming. To that child the Lord of Life,
the Ruler of Heaven, gave worldly honor.
So Scyld's son Beow[3] himself won fame,
his glory spread wide among nations of the North.
The young man did as he ought, won good will,   20
while under his father he gave out great gifts,
so that his dear comrades, when he became king,
would then stand by him, as steadfast retainers,
when war came. By such deeds of honor
shall a man prosper among all the peoples.[4]   25

---

*Legendary founder of the Danish royal line; pronounced "Shild Shefing," since in Old English /sc/ is pronounced as our "sh."

Then still full of strength, at his fated time,
Scyld passed away, left for the Lord's keeping.
Friends bore him out to the flow of the sea,
as he had earlier directed his dear comrades,
while as lord of the Scyldings he still wielded words,   30
the long-loved ruler over the broad realm.
There at the harbor stood a ring-prowed ship,
icy and eager to set out, a nobleman's vessel.
Then they laid down the beloved leader,
their renowned ring-giver, in the bosom of the ship[5]   35
next to the mast. There was a mass of treasures,
wealth brought there from far-away lands.
Nor have I heard of a ship more splendidly laden
with weapons for battle and dress for war,
with swords and shirts of mail. On his breast lay   40
many of these treasures, to travel with him
through the mighty power of the plunging sea.
Nor did they give to him any lesser gifts,
from the people's treasures, than did those
who, at the first, had sent him forth,   45
alone as a child, over the stretch of the sea.
Next they set over him a golden standard,
high over his head, and let the tide bear him off,
out over the ocean. Sad were the people,
mindful of mourning. Nor, to speak truth,   50
do any men know—among wise advisors,
those heroes under the heavens—who received that cargo.

— I[*]—

Then was Beow of the Scyldings a beloved king
for a long time, in the town-forts of the people,
famed among the folk—his father had passed on,   55
that king gone from his home—till to Beow was born
Healfdene the High, who nobly ruled the Scyldings
as long as he lived, old and battle-fierce.
To that wise ruler, the leader of warriors,
children awoke into the world, four altogether: 60
Heorogar and Hrothgar and Halga the Good,
and I heard that [. . . was On]ela's queen,[6]
dear bed-fellow of the Heatho-Scylfing king.

    Then was bold Hrothgar given battle-success,
honor in warfare, so his comrades in combat   65
followed him eagerly, until the youths grew
to a great warrior band. To his mind came a plan
that he would order a hall to be built:
they would raise on high a great mead-hall[7]
whose fame would forever be heard among men;   70
there from within he would deal out,
both to young and to old, all that God gave him—
except common land and men's life blood.
Then I have heard that many among nations,
throughout this middle-earth, were mustered to work,   75
to adorn the high hall as a place for the people.
As men reckon time, it was all ready with speed,
the greatest of hall-buildings. Hrothgar the king,
who wielded power with words, named the
    hall Heorot.
He fulfilled his pledge, dealt out precious rings,   80

---

*The manuscript uses Roman numerals for sections called "fitts."

treasures at the feast. The great hall towered,
high and horn-vaulted—yet awaiting hostile flames,
a most hateful fire. For it would not be long
till sword-heat between son-in-law and father-in-law,
would waken their feud after deadly hatred.[8]   85
    Then a fierce evil demon suffered distress,
long in torment, who dwelt in darkness.
For day after day, he heard rejoicing
loud in the hall: there was music of the harp,
and clear song of the scop,[9] who sang of creation,   90
the beginnings of men far back in time.
He proclaimed the Almighty created the earth,
a land of beauty, surrounded by seas;
the Triumphant One made the sun and the moon
as lights to shine on all land-dwellers,   95
and clothed the corners of the world
with limbs and leaves, and created life
for every kind of the quick who stir with life.
Thus did loyal men live their lives in joy,
happy in the hall, till that one began   100
to work his wickedness, a fiend from hell.
Grendel was the name of this ghastly stranger,
famed wanderer in wastelands, who held the moors,
the fens and fastnesses. Once this unhappy beast
dwelt in the country of monstrous creatures,   105
after the Creator had condemned all those
among Cain's kin—the eternal Lord
avenged the crime of the one who killed Abel.
For Cain got no joy from committing that wrong,
but God banished him far away from mankind.   110
From him all wicked offspring were born:
giants and elves, and evil demon-creatures,
and gigantic monsters—those who fought God,
time beyond time. But God repaid them!

— II —

When night grew dark, Grendel sought out   115
the high hall, to see how the Ring-Danes
after beer-drinking had settled to bed.
He found within a noble warrior-band,
asleep after feasting; they knew not sorrow,
the misery of men. The wicked creature,   120
grim and greedy, was at the ready,
savage and cruel, and seized in their rest
thirty of the thanes.* He then went from there,
exulting in spoils, to seek his own home,
to find his dwelling, with his fill of slaughter.   125
        Then in the dawn, with the break of day,
Grendel's war-strength was made known to men.
After the night's feasting, a lament now rose up,
great cry in the morning. The glorious king,
as always a noble, sat full of sorrow,   130
the great one grieving over his lost thanes.
Soon after they saw foot-tracks of their foe,
the cursed stranger. That struggle had been too strong,
too loathsome and long-lasting! Nor was there respite,
but after one night, Grendel once more committed   135
yet more murderous slaughter. He mourned not
for his horrid deeds: he was too bent on those.
Then was it easy to find one who elsewhere
sought far-away for his place of rest,
his bed in an out-building—when danger became clear,   140
as the truth was told by signs of the terror,
the hatred of this hall-stalker. Thus he held himself
far-off and more safe by escaping the fiend.

---

*Noble retainers of a king or great lord.

So Grendel held sway and fought against right,
alone against all, till the best of houses   145
was left idle. A long time passed,
twelve winters all-told, while the lord of the Scyldings
endured great grief, every kind of woe,
a surging of sorrows. Thus to the nations,
both far and wide, it became known   150
through tales sadly sung, that Grendel fought
a long while against Hrothgar—waged his terrors,
wicked and fearsome, for many half-years*
in unending strife. He did not desire peace
with any warrior of the Danish host,   155
nor to lift the life-threat in return for payment.
None of the Scyldings could surely expect
fair compensation from the killer's hands,
but the horrid monster, a dark death-shadow,
harried the heroes, laid in wait to ambush   160
both warriors and youths. He held through the night
the moors thick with mist, and men knew not
where that hell-demon would glide in his wanderings.
Thus again and again, this foe of mankind,
this friendless horror, carried out a host of crimes,   165
of hard humiliations. He held sway in Heorot,
the brilliant hall, in the black of night;
yet could not come near the rich gift-throne,
protected by God, not knowing God's love.

That was much misery for the lord of the Scyldings,   170
near breaking of spirit. Many noble Danes
sat often in council to consider what advice
was best for the band of strong-hearted warriors
to defend against sudden attacks of terror.
For a time they prayed in heathen temples,   175

---

*The early peoples of the North reckoned time in half-years or in winters.

worshipping idols, and pleading with words
for the Slayer of Souls to come to their aid
in the nation's crisis. Such then was their custom,
the hope of heathens; in their hearts
they bore hell, they knew not the Creator, 180
the Judge of all deeds—neither acknowledged the Lord,
nor knew how to praise the Protector of Heaven,
the Ruler of Glory. Woe be to the one,
who through terrible sin, would shove his soul
into the fire's embrace, foregoing all hope, 185
with no chance of change! Happy the one,
who after his death-day, may seek the Ruler
for peace and protection in the Father's arms.[10]

— III —

Because of this horror, the son of Healfdene
seethed with sorrow, nor might the wise hero 190
put aside woe. That struggle was too strong,
hateful and long-lasting, which had come on the people,
dire wrack and ruin—the greatest of night-evils.

In his own homeland, the thane of Hygelac,*
the valiant Geat, heard the tales told of Grendel. 195
This Geat was among men the greatest in strength,
most noble and mighty, for as long as his life-days
were destined to last. He directed a wave-traveler
to be well prepared, and said he would seek
the Danish war-king, that renowned ruler, 200
over the swan-road,† since the Dane was in need.
The wise men of the Geats could find no fault

---

*This is Beowulf, son of Ecgtheow; pronounced "Edge-theow," since Old English /cg/
is pronounced as our "j."
†A kenning for the sea (a kenning is the combined use of two nouns or phrases to
create a metaphor that stands for some person or thing).

with that journey, though their hero to them was dear:
they inspected the omens and urged on the brave one.
This excellent chieftain had chosen as comrades   205
the best and the bravest from among the Geats
that he might find. With these fourteen
he sought the sea-planks, a skillful sailor,
leading the way down to the end of the land.
The time was ready, with the ship on the waves,   210
the boat beneath cliffs. Well-equipped young warriors
stepped up on the prow. Sea-currents wound round,
sea against sand. Then the warriors bore
into the ship's bosom the shining war-gear,
their splendid arms. The men shoved off   215
the well-bound vessel, for the much-sought voyage.
The foamy-necked boat, most like a bird,
soared over the waves, made eager by wind—
until in due time, the following day,
the tightly-wound prow had traveled so far   220
that the seafarers now sighted the land:
shining shore-cliffs, the towering banks,
the broad headlands. The boat crossed the waters,
to the end of the sea. Then swiftly they rose.
Men of the Weders* mounted up on the shore,   225
made fast the wood vessel, and shook their mail-shirts,
their armor for war. Then they thanked God
that the path through the waves was easily passed.

    High on the cliff, the Danes' coastguard watched,
charged with protecting the borders by the sea.   230
As he saw strangers bear bright shields from their ship,
armor ready for use, curiosity pressed into his thoughts,
as he wondered just what these strange men were.
He went right to the shore riding on his horse,

---

*Another name for the Geats.

this thane of Hrothgar, and shook the great spear   235
he held in his hand, while with formal words he asked:
"What bold men are you, thus bearing your arms,
protected by mail, who have made such a journey
in a tall ship traversing the sea-road,
to come here over the waves? Hear me! I have long   240
been guard of the coast, held watch by the sea,
so no hateful enemy might launch an attack
with a ship-army in the land of the Scyldings.
Never have shield-bearers come to these shores
more openly than you. Nor could you be sure   245
of words of welcome from our war-leaders,
consent from our kinsmen. Never have I seen
a greater earl on the earth than one of you,
a man in his war-gear. He is no hall-retainer,
ennobled with weapons, unless his looks belie him,   250
given his peerless form. Now, I must press you,
to know your lineage, lest you venture forth,
any farther from here, as enemy spies
into the land of the Danes. Now, you far-dwellers,
you seafaring men who have come as strangers,   255
hear my plain thought: haste would be best
for you to make known your home and your nation."

— IV —

The chief among those seamen made answer,
the war-band leader unlocked his word-hoard:
"We have come from the country of the Geats,   260
and are hearth-companions of Hygelac.
My father was well known among the nations,
a noble chieftain, Ecgtheow by name.
He weathered many winters till he passed away,
an old man from his homeland; every one of the wise   265

throughout the wide earth remembers him well.
In friendly spirit we have come here to seek
your own high ruler, the son of Healfdene,
protector of his people. May you give us good counsel!
We have come on a quest to that famous one,   270
the king of the Danes: nothing will be concealed,
held back when we meet. Now you must know,
if it has been told truly, as we have heard,
that a foe of the Scyldings—of what sort I know not—
a mysterious hate-dealer, with terror displays   275
unthinkable evil during dark nights,
humiliation and slaughter. So for this I seek
to counsel Hrothgar in heart-felt friendship,
how the wise and good king, may overcome
        the fiend—
if ever relief should come to reverse   280
the terrible affliction of all these evils—
and his surges of sorrow then become cooler.
Or else ever after he will suffer distress,
a terrible fate, while towering on high
the best of halls will remain without joy."   285
        The guardian spoke, seated on horseback,
a fearless captain: "A shrewd shield-warrior
must judge the meanings of each of two things,
of words and of works, if he thinks clearly.
I hear and judge that this is a force friendly   290
to the lord of the Scyldings. You have my leave
to go forth bearing weapons. I will guide you.
And I shall bid my band of young thanes
to guard with honors against all enemies
your sea-going vessel, the new-tarred ship   295
there on the sand—until once again it bears
its noble seafarer over streams of the deep,
in the wound-wood prow to the land of the Weders,

a good people, as it may be granted by fate
that through the battle-storm he may safely pass."   300
With him they went forth. Their vessel stayed,
the broad-bosomed ship, at rest on its ropes,
held fast by an anchor. Images of boars shone
over helmet cheek-guards glowing with gold,
flashing and fire-hard—the war-minded boar watched   305
over life for the grim ones.[11] The men made haste,
marching together, till they might see
the timbered hall, grand and gold-adorned,
the greatest of buildings among earth-dwellers,
of all under heaven. That hall housed the mighty king,   310
its light shining far over many lands.
The battle-brave coastguard pointed out to them
the splendid hall, so they might themselves
go directly there. Then this Danish warrior
turned round his steed, and spoke these words: 315
"The time has come for me to go. May the almighty
Father favor you with help, and grant to you
a safe venture. I return to the sea
to hold my watch against hostile foes."

— V —

The way was cobbled, and it guided the men   320
marching together. The war-mail shone,
the bright iron rings linked hard by hand,
so the battle-gear sang. Thus they proceeded,
in their awesome arms, to go to the hall.
The sea-weary men set down their broad shields,   325
with the powerful bosses, by the side of the hall.
As the men sat on a bench, the mail rang out,
the battle-shirts of heroes. Their spears stood tall,
the weapons of warriors all gathered together,

a grove of ash-woods gray at their tips. That company
    of iron   330
was honored with weapons!
                       Then a proud Dane
questioned these warriors about their origin:
"From what place do you bear these gold-plated shields,
these gray shirts of mail and sheltering helmets,
this stock of battle-shafts? I am Hrothgar's   335
herald and attendant. Never have I seen
so many foreign men more brave in their bearing.
I think you seek Hrothgar—not in haughty pride,
nor as exiles without homes, but for greatness of heart."
The one famed for strength, proud chief of the Weders,   340
answered the attendant, speaking formal words
with force from his helmet: "We are Hygelac's
drinking-bowl companions. Beowulf is my name.
I wish to speak to the son of Healfdene,
the renowned king, your own great ruler,   345
about my goal in coming, if he will grant
that we may meet with such a gracious lord."
Then spoke Hrothgar's herald, Wulfgar the Wendel,
whose honor was known among many men,
with his valor and wisdom: "I will go in to the king   350
to discuss with the friend and lord of the Danes,
the lord of the Scyldings, giver of great rings,
regarding your venture as you request;
and his reply I will make known right away,
whatever he wishes to give you in answer."   355
      The herald went quickly to where Hrothgar sat,
old and most hoary, among his band of earls.
That one famed for courage stood before the shoulders
of the Danish lord; he knew well the customs of the court.
Wulfgar spoke to his well-loved leader: 360
"To us from afar over the sea's expanse

men have come from the homeland of the Geats.
The warriors call their chief comrade-in-arms
Beowulf by name. They bid that you may grant,
my generous lord, that with you they may 365
have concourse with words. Do not refuse this request
in the answer you give, gracious Hrothgar!
Dressed in their war-gear, they appear worthy
of the honor of earls. Their chief is specially strong,
who led these warriors to our land." 370

— VI —

Hrothgar spoke, protector of the Scyldings:
"I have known this one since he was a boy.
His father was known by the name of Ecgtheow,
to whom Hrethel of the Geats gave in marriage
his only daughter. His son has now 375
boldly come here to seek out a faithful friend.
It is said among many seafaring men
who have taken treasures to the Geats as gifts
for thanks to that people—that this one has
won fame in fighting, with thirty men's might 380
in the grip of his hand. The holy God
has sent him to help our people of the
West-Danes, so we may have hope
against the dread of Grendel. For his daring
I shall give great gifts to this good man. 385
Go in haste and bid these guests come in
to see our kinsmen, comrades gathered together.
Speak to them these words—that they are welcome
among the people of the Danes." [Then to the door
went the honored herald]* to speak words from within: 390

---

*Official of Hrothgar's court.

"My victorious leader, the lord of the East Danes,
bids me tell you that he knows your lineage,
and that you brave men who have come to him
over the sea-surgings are welcome here.
Now you may go wearing your war-gear,   395
with heads under helmets, in to see Hrothgar.
You shall leave here at rest your battle-shields,
and your wooden spears, while words are exchanged."
        The mighty Geat arose, and warriors with him,
a brave band of thanes. Some remained in place,   400
guards over war-gear, as directed by their leader.
They quickly went, as the herald led the way,
under Hrothgar's hall-roof. [The hero strode,]
stern under helmet, till he stood on the hearth.
Then Beowulf spoke—on him the armor shone,   405
the mail-shirt linked by skills of the smith:
"Hail to you, Hrothgar! I am Hygelac's kinsman
and devoted thane; already in youth I have done
many glorious deeds. Tales about Grendel
have come to my ears in my own homeland.   410
Seafaring men have said that this hall,
the best of buildings, stands idle and useless
for all you warriors, after the light of evening
becomes hidden under the cover of heaven.
Then those known in my nation as the very best   415
among the wise counselors, gave me advice
to look for ways to help you, Lord Hrothgar,
since they knew the power of my strength—
for they had watched when from battles I came,
stained with blood of foes: once I bound five,   420
destroyed the kin of giants; and in the sea slew
water-monsters at night while in dire distress;
won vengeance for Weders, ground down hateful foes—
those asked for woe. And now with Grendel,

that horrid demon, I shall hold alone   425
a meeting with the monster. Thus, of you,
chief among Bright-Danes, protector of Scyldings,
I wish to ask for one favor, in the fervent hope
that you not refuse me—O ruler of warriors,
O dear friend of the folk—since I have come from afar: 430
that I alone, with my band of bold comrades,
these brave warriors here, may cleanse Heorot.
I have asked and have learned that this monster,
in his reckless folly, forswears using weapons.
Therefore, so that my lord Hygelac may have   435
pride in my venture, I will myself scorn
to bear a sword, or a broad yellow shield,
to wage this battle. But I shall hand-to-hand
grapple with this demon, and fight to the death,
foe against foe. There one must trust the judgment   440
of God as to which is carried away by death.
I expect Grendel will, if he may wield power
over bold men of the Geats in the battle-hall,
feed on the flesh of his enemies,
as he has often done. There will be no need   445
to cover my head, but he will have me,
dripping with blood, if death bears me off.
He will carry the corpse to gobble the gore,
this lone-going creature, greedy in eating,
drooling in the moors. You need not be moved   450
to fret for long over this feeding on me.
If the battle bears me off, send to Hygelac
the best of war-garments defending my breast,
the hard linked mail—left to me by Hrethel,
the work of Weland. Wyrd* goes ever as it must!"   455

---

*In Scandinavian, Anglo-Saxon, and German legend, Weland is a weapon-smith of
great skill. Wyrd is the Anglo-Saxon name for the force of fate.

— VII —

Hrothgar spoke, king of the Scyldings:
"For past deeds done and for past support
you have sought to find us, my friend Beowulf.
Once your father brought about a great feud
when he killed Heatholaf with his own hand   460
among the Wulfings, and his kin in the Weders
refused him protection for fear of war.
From there he sought the folk of the South-Danes,
us Honor-Scyldings, over the rolling waves.
I was then first ruling the folk of the Danes   465
wielding power in my youth over wide-spread lands,
with a stronghold of warriors. Heorogar was then dead,
my elder brother, from our father Healfdene,
was no longer living—a better man than I!
I then paid to settle the feud for your father.   470
I sent to the Wulfings over welling waters
ancient treasures, and Ecgtheow swore oaths to me.[12]
I now suffer great sorrow in spirit to say,
before any man, what Grendel has brought
to humiliate Heorot with his hateful schemes   475
and his horrid attacks. My hall-troop dwindles,
now less of a war-band. Wyrd swept them off
in the terror of Grendel. May God quickly
cut off that mad pillager from power to act!
Often our warriors, when over their ale-cups,   480
made boasts during beer-drinking
that they in the beer-hall would wait and watch
to do battle with Grendel, wielding dread swords.
Then in the morning was this mead-hall
stained with their blood in the break of day: 485
all the hall-benches were steaming hot gore,

from the slaughter in the hall. Still less did I have
of well-loved warriors as death carried them off.
Now sit down to the feast and unfasten your thoughts
to these gallant men, as your spirit moves you." 490
    Then in the beer-hall were benches cleared
for the Geats as a group all gathered together.
Their strong chieftain went over to take his seat,
famed for his strength. A thane performed service,
who bore in his hands the adorned ale-cup, 495
and poured out sweet drink. At times the scop sang,
a clear voice in Heorot. There was joy among heroes,
the roar of retainers, of Danes and of Weders.

— VIII —

    Unferth[13] then spoke, the son of Ecglaf,
who sat at the feet of the lord of the Scyldings, 500
brought forth fighting words—for to him the venture
of brave seafaring Beowulf was great offence,
since he could not stand that any other man
might earn more glory throughout middle-earth,
under the heavens, than he himself: 505
"Are you the Beowulf who with Breca competed,
on the broad sea in a swimming contest,
where out of bravado you dared ocean-danger,
and for foolish boasting gambled your lives
in the ocean deep? Nor might any man, 510
either friend or foe, dissuade you from
that perilous plan. You two swam out on the sea,
your strong arms embracing the streams,
crossing the sea-paths, coursing with hands,
gliding over ocean. Waves welled up, 515
the wildness of winter. You both in the water's power
struggled seven nights, till he surpassed you at sea,

proved stronger in swimming. Then currents at dawn
carried him to the coast of the Heatho-Raemas,
and from there he sought his own native soil,   520
the land of the Brondings with its bright stronghold,
where beloved Breca ruled over his nation,
both towns and treasures. This son of Beanstan
thus truly fulfilled his boast to beat you.
And so I expect still worse of an outcome—   525
though elsewhere you were bold in battle-storms,
fierce in the fighting—if you dare a whole night
to wait here for Grendel, the grisly monster."
        Then Beowulf spoke, the son of Ecgtheow,
"Well, my friend Unferth, besotted with beer,   530
you have brought forth much about Breca,
told tales of his venture! Yet I tell the truth,
that I have proved greater in sea-strength,
more of a match for the waves, than any other man.
While we were still boys, we two agreed   535
and made great boasts—as may often pass
between youths—that out on the sea we both
would dare the deep, and so that we did.
As we swam out to sea, we held near at hand
our naked swords, steeled to fend off   540
whales in the water. He might not swim
away from me with swifter speed in the sea,
amid boiling waves, nor did I leave him behind.
We two stayed together in welling waters
for five full nights, till driven apart by rising swells,   545
by walls of water in the fiercest of weathers.
The night grew dark, and winds from the north
attacked us in battle, the waves wild warriors.
Monsters of the deep were roused to rage.
Against these foes, my strong mail-shirt,   550
with links forged by hand, woven for war,

served as defense where it kept my breast safe,
glowing with gold. One dreaded foe drew me
down to the deep, holding me fast
in its gruesome grip. Yet to me it was given   555
that I struck the sea-monster with the point of my sword,
a blade proved in battle. Thus through my hand,
the storm of my sword swept the beast away.

— IX —

"Again and again, these loathsome creatures
pressed me severely—though I served them well   560
with my fine old sword, as it was fitting.
By no means did these wicked destroyers
have the joy of feasting, tasting my flesh,
while seated to dine at the bottom of the sea.
But in the morning, those struck by my blade   565
were cast up on the shore, the leavings of waves,
slain by the sword, so never thereafter
did they threaten the journeys of seafaring men
over deep water-ways. Light came from the east,
bright beacon of God. And the waves subsided,   570
so I might see the towering sea-nesses,
the windy high walls. Wyrd often preserves
one not doomed to die, if his courage is strong!
It thus fell to me that I with the sword
slew nine sea-foes. Never have I heard   575
under heaven's arch of a harder night-battle,
nor of a man more sore-pressed among streams of waves.
Still, I survived from those hostile grasps,
worn-out from the struggles. Then the sea bore me,
in a rushing current of welling waters,   580
to the land of the Finns. Never have I heard
such stories told of your skill in battle,

in furious sword-fights. Never yet has Breca—
nor either of you two—done deeds
of such blood-sport so boldly in battle,   585
with burnished blades—nor here do I boast—
yet you have killed your own brothers,
your nearest kin. For that you shall suffer
the horrors of hell, though your wit be sharp.
I therefore say to you truly, son of Ecglaf,   590
that never would Grendel, that gruesome monster,
have taken such a toll on your lord and men,
humiliating Heorot, if your spirit were
so fierce in battle as you suppose yourself.
But Grendel has learned not to fear a feud,   595
or serious sword-storm, from your people,
nor to tremble in terror at the Victory-Scyldings.
He strikes at will, not sparing even one
of the men of the Danes, but fills his desire
for death and devouring among the Spear-Danes,   600
without fear of fighting. But now before long,
I shall show to him the strength and courage
of Geats in warfare. Then the one who still can
will go bravely to the mead, when morning's sun,
clothed in light, shall shine from the south   605
over children of men for another day."
      Then there was joy for the giver of treasures,
gray-haired and battle-brave. The chief of the Bright-Danes,
protector of his people, now counted on help,
for he heard in the hero a resolute purpose.   610
      There was the laughter of heroes, a happy uproar
rejoicing in shouts. Then Wealhtheow stepped forth,
mindful of courtesy. The queen of Hrothgar,
adorned with gold, greeted the men in the hall.
The noble woman first offered the ale-cup   615
to the lord of the land of the East-Danes.

She bade him have joy in the drinking of beer,
dear to his followers, and the king famed for victory
took all he desired from the feast and the hall-cup.
Then the lady of the Helmings* went all around,   620
to men and youths, serving each a share
in precious cups—till the time came
that the gold-adorned queen, in a gracious spirit,
bore the mead-cup directly to Beowulf.
Wise in words, she greeted the Geats' prince,   625
thanking God for granting her greatest wish
that now she could trust in one truly noble
to halt wicked attacks. The battle-fierce warrior
took the cup held in Wealhtheow's hands
and related to her his readiness for battle.   630
Beowulf spoke, the son of Ecgtheow:
"I was determined, when I set out to sea,
seated in sailing-boat with my band of warriors,
that I would completely fulfill the wish
of your people, or fall in the fight,   635
in the grasp of Grendel. I shall perform
great deeds of valor, or I shall see
the last day of my life in this mead-hall."
The queen liked well these fearless words,
the Geat's boasting-speech. Adorned with gold,   640
the noble wife went to sit by her lord.

    Then, once again, inside the hall
were brave words spoken by spirited people,
the sounds of happiness—till the time came
when the son of Healfdene wished to seek   645
rest for the night. For the king knew the monster
was bent on battle in the high hall,
once men might not see the light of the sun,

---

*Queen Wealhtheow.

with night growing dark over all the earth,
and shapes of shadows came gliding along,   650
dark under clouds. The company all rose up.
Then Hrothgar addressed himself to Beowulf,
warrior to warrior, and wished him success,
power over the wine-hall, speaking formal words:
"Never before, since I could lift hand and shield,   655
have I given care of the great hall of the Danes
to any other man, as I now do to you.
Now have and hold this best of dwellings,
mindful of glory, and make known your might,
guard against fierce foes. Nor will you lack reward   660
if you survive the great task before you."

— X —

Then Hrothgar went out with his band of heroes,
the protector of the Danes departed the hall.
This war-chief wished to seek out Wealhtheow,
his queen and bed-fellow. As men have heard,   665
the glorious ruler had set a hall-guard
against the foe Grendel—serving special duty
for the king of the Danes, keeping watch against giants.
Truly, the prince of the Geats firmly trusted
in the force of his strength and the favor of God.   670
   He then shook off his shirt of iron mail
and helmet from his head. He gave to another
his burnished sword, the best iron for battle,
and ordered him to hold this war-gear for now.
Then the bold man, Beowulf of the Geats,   675
spoke words of boasting before mounting his bed:
"I do not suppose myself any less battle-bold,
or less strong in the struggle than Grendel himself,
so I will not put him to sleep with a sword,

to rob him of life, though I readily could.   680
He knows not of weapons—how to strike with sword,
how to hew my shield—though he is renowned
for his furious fighting. No, we two in dark of night
shall forego the sword, if he dares to seek
war without weapon, and then may wise God,   685
the holy Lord, judge which side will succeed,
which one will win glory, as to him seems right."
Then the battle-brave Geat reclined, lay his face
on a cushion, and courageous sea-men
lay on their hall-beds all around him.   690
Not one of them thought that from that place
he might ever again return to his homeland,
come to his kin or the town where he was reared.
For they had heard that death had destroyed
far too great a number of the Danish folk   695
in that wine-hall. Yet God gave to them,
this band of Weders, good fortune in war,
strong help and support—so they could defeat
the fearsome foe through one man's skill,
his own great might. Thus the truth is made known   700
that almighty God has always wielded power
over the nations of men.
                              Then in the dark of the night
came the shadow-glider. The warriors were sleeping
who were appointed to guard the gabled hall—
all except one. It was known to the men   705
that the dread demon could not throw them
down in the darkness when God did not wish it.
But the one who was watching with spirit enraged
awaited the outcome of fighting this foe.

— XI —

Then from the moors that were thick with mist,   710
Grendel emerged, wrapped in the anger of God.
The hellish ravager sought to surprise
one of the men at rest in the high hall.
He crept under clouds toward the wine-hall,
till he could see clearly the glorious building,   715
glowing with gold plates. Nor was this
the first time he sought Hrothgar's home,
yet never before or after, in all his days,
did he find a worse fortune among the hall-thanes.
Then deprived of joy, the creature came   720
to the famed hall. When touched by his hands,
the door sprang open, burst from its bands.
Then bent on destruction, and bulging with rage,
he forced open the hall's mouth to move quickly in—
a fiend trespassing on the shining floor,   725
his spirit filled with fire. His eyes shone forth
with fearsome lights much like flames.
He saw in the hall a large group of heroes,
a company of kinsmen all sleeping together,
a brave band of warriors. His spirit exulted   730
as the monster expected, before break of day,
to tear life from limbs of everyone there,
wreaking his terror while harvesting hope
of feasting on flesh. Yet it was not his fate
that he might again feed on the race of men,   735
after that night. The heroic kinsman of Hygelac
closely watched how the wicked man-slayer
fought with such skill in sudden attacks.
Nor did the demon think to delay,
but for his first victim he swiftly seized   740

a sleeping warrior and slit him wide open,
biting into the body, drinking blood in streams,
swallowing huge mouthfuls—till soon
he had eaten the entire man's corpse,
even feet and hands. Next he stepped forth 745
to clutch with his claws strong-hearted Beowulf
where he lay at rest, the foe reaching for him
to grab with his hands. The Geat answered quickly,
propped on one arm, he faced the attack.
That devourer of men then soon discovered 750
that he never had met any one in middle-earth,
even in far-off regions, of the race of men
with hand-grip more strong. His spirit sank,
filled with fear that he could not get away.
He was eager for flight, to escape into darkness, 755
to find fellowship with devils. Never had he met
such a dread encounter in his former days.
The brave kinsman of Hygelac then brought to mind
his speech last evening and sprang to his feet,
to hold his foe fast till his fingers broke. 760
The giant fought to flee, but the Geat still advanced.
The wicked destroyer wildly thought
where to make his escape, far away from the hall,
to find safety in fens, yet knew his fingers trapped
in his enemy's grasp. This was a grim journey 765
that the hellish ravager took to Heorot!
The din filled the mead-hall. All of the Danes,
the bold warriors, were to drink this time
the ale of terror. Both fighters raged in their fury,
as they fought for the hall. The tall house trembled. 770
It was a great wonder that the wine-hall,
the fairest of buildings, withstood the war-strife,
did not fall to the ground. But it was held firm,
from both within and without, by iron bands

skillfully fastened. Many a mead-bench,   775
adorned with gold, flew from the floor,
as I have heard told, in the struggle of foes.
No wise warrior among the Scyldings
would have thought any man could by his own might
so threaten to destroy the hall decked with horns,   780
to break it apart—though it might fall in fire's embrace,
swallowed in smoke. New sounds rose up
that were not of this earth. The North-Danes recoiled
at the horrible terror, as each of their troop
heard a wail go up from inside the walls,   785
the enemy of God screaming songs of despair,
his cries of defeat—as this captive of hell
found his wounds fatal. Beowulf won with his death-grip,
proved the greatest in might of any man,
in that day and time, during his life on earth.   790

— XII —

    This protector of warriors did not at all wish
to let loose the death-bringer while still alive,
nor did he count Grendel's life-days of value
to anyone at all. There many a man of Beowulf's band
eagerly brandished their ancient sword-blades,   795
wishing to protect the life of their lord,
the widely famed chief, any way that they could.
While engaged in the fray, these brave-minded warriors
sought to strike at the foe from every side,
but could not figure how to hew Grendel down,   800
how to seek out his soul: nor might any war-sword,
not the strongest of irons in all of the earth,
even touch to do harm to that evil destroyer—
for Grendel wove spells round all human weapons,
on all swords of victory. Yet severed from life,   805

he was fated to feel misery at the end of his days,
his time on the earth, and the alien terror must now
embark on a far journey into the power of fiends.

    Then that one found out, who so often before
had wrought wicked evils, terrified the spirits   810
of the race of men—he waged war against God—
that this time his fearsome strength would fail him,
for his high-spirited foe, the kinsman of Hygelac,
held him fast by the hand. Each hated the other,
while they both lived. The dreaded demon   815
suffered terrible torture, as his shoulder tore open,
a great wound gaping as sinews sprang apart,
and the bone-locks burst. To Beowulf then
was glory given in battle. Sick unto death,
Grendel could only flee to the fen-slopes,   820
seek his home without joy. He certainly knew
that he had reached the length of his life,
his number of days. But for all of the Danes
joy was renewed after the onslaught of death.
The hero from afar, the kinsman of Hygelac,   825
shrewd and strong hearted, cleansed Hrothgar's hall,
saved it from sorrow. He rejoiced in his night-work,
a champion's great deeds. The prince of the Geats
had fulfilled his boast to the folk of the East-Danes,
had completely relieved them from heaviness of heart,   830
from sorrow caused by evils that they long endured,
from the horrible menace they were forced to suffer,
from no little affliction. That was a true trophy
which the battle-brave Beowulf set down before them,
under the hall-roof—the hand, arm, and shoulder,   835
with Grendel's claw, all connected together.

— XIII —

Then in the morning, as I have heard,
in the gift-hall many a warrior gathered,
the chiefs of the folk, from near and from far,
traveled the wide roads to look on the wonder,　　　840
the tracks of the demon. Nor did it occur
to any of the warriors who saw those steps
that they should grieve for this one without glory—
how weary in spirit, he went on his way,
beaten in battle, put to flight by fate,　　　845
left a trail of life-blood to the mere of monsters.
There with blood the water was welling,
horrid surging of waves all swirling together,
heated with gore, and gushing battle-blood.
The one doomed to die, without any joy,　　　850
sought to hide in the fens, and laid down his life,
the soul of a heathen to be taken by hell.
From that awful scene went the old retainers,
joined by the youths, all joyful together.
High-spirited men rode horses from the mere,　　　855
bold on their mounts. There was Beowulf's
glory proclaimed. Many a man often declared
that in the north or the south, between the two seas,
throughout the whole earth, under expanse of the sky,
there was no one better among shield-bearing men—　　　860
no greater warrior more worthy of a kingdom.
Yet they found no blame in their own friendly lord,
their gracious Hrothgar, for he was a good king.
At times the bold ones let their steeds leap forward,
urged their glossy horses to compete in contests,　　　865
over ground they found fitting for holding the races,
known as good tracks. Also there was a thane,

well-loaded with words and filled with old tales,
who had a great store of traditional stories,
in memory retained—yet could make a new tale   870
based on true new events. And so he began
to sing with skill of Beowulf's adventure
and with masterful talent to perform his tale,
in words well-woven. He related all things
he had ever heard told of the legendary deeds   875
of Sigemund*—many stories till now unsung—
the fights of Waels' son, his far journeys,
the feuds and wickedness that were not well known
to the sons of men. Yet Sigemund would tell
somewhat of these things to Fitela by his side,   880
uncle to nephew, as comrades in crises,
ever faithful together in fights against foes,
having laid low a great many of the kin of giants
with their strong swords. So the fame of Sigemund
spread far and wide after his death-day   885
since the battle-bold hero defeated the dragon,
the guard of a hoard. Under gray rocks
this son of a chieftain took his chances alone,
a daring deed—nor was Fitela then with him.
Yet to him it was given to stab with his sword   890
through the wondrous dragon, clear into the wall,
where the iron stuck. Thus was the dragon slain.
The warrior won the prize by his boldness,
so he now could enjoy the hoard of treasures,
however he wished. The son of Waels   895
then loaded the sea-boat, bore to the ship's bosom
the shining wealth—while the dragon melted in flames.
      He was by far the most famous of heroes,
among all the nations, for his noble deeds

---

*A great hero in Northern European legends, the son of Waels.

as protector of warriors—for that he prospered—   900
outshining Heremod whose glory grew less,[14]
in strength and bravery. Heremod was betrayed,
while among the Jutes, into the power of enemies
and quickly slain. The surgings of sorrow
had long made him weaker among his warriors   905
as he had become the source of their suffering.
For often before, in earlier times, many a wise man
bemoaned the course of that strong-minded king,
had trusted in him as their relief from torments,
that he as their prince would have favor of fortune,   910
to follow his father as king over the people,
holding treasure and stronghold in that land of heroes,
the home of the Scyldings. In contrast to him,
Beowulf became to the Danes and all mankind
a far greater friend—while Heremod waded in evil.   915
    At times, retainers competed by racing with horses
along the dirt road. Well beyond dawn, the morning-light
had hastened forward. And many strong-minded men
proceeded onward to reach the high hall
to see the curious wonder; and the king himself,   920
the guardian of treasures, great in his glory,
and famed for his bounty, walked from his wife's chamber
with his band of warriors—and with him his queen
went to the mead-hall with her own troop of maidens.

— XIV —

    Hrothgar spoke, when he arrived at the hall,   925
standing on a step, looked up to the high roof
adorned with gold and with Grendel's hand:
"For this sight let us give thanks at once
to the Ruler of All. I have endured many afflictions,
griefs caused by Grendel. Ever may God work   930

wonder after wonder, as Guardian of the world.
Not long ago, I had no reason to hope
that I might receive remedy as long as I lived
from any of these woes, while the best of halls
stood stained with blood, gory from battle—   935
misery spread wide among all the wise counselors,
who dared not hope they might ever defend
their fortified home from hateful foes,
wicked spirits and demons. Now has a warrior
performed that deed through the power of the Lord,   940
which until this time none of us could contrive
how to do it ourselves. Hail to the woman
who may say, if still living, that she gave birth
to such a son among all the peoples of earth,
that the Ancient Ruler bestowed a great gift   945
in the birth of her child. Now I tell you, Beowulf,
the best of men, I wish you for my son
with heart-felt love—to hold from now on
in new bond of kinship. Nor will you lack any
of the worldly goods that I have the power to give.   950
Often for lesser deeds I have handed out rewards,
prizes of hoard-treasures, to a more lowly man,
one weaker in fighting. Yet you have yourself,
performed such feats that your fame shall live
for ever and ever. May the Ruler of All   955
reward your great goodness, as he has so far."
    Then Beowulf spoke, the son of Ecgtheow:
"We have fought the fight, the test of courage,
with much good will, braving with boldness
unknown monstrous might. I would rather that you   960
could have seen Grendel himself with your own eyes,
the foe in his war-gear falling weary unto death!
As quickly as I could, I tried with strong grips
to bind him down to a bed of slaughter

so that he in the powerful hold of my hands   965
would lie in death-torment, lest his body slip away.
Yet the Maker of All did not wish that I might
hinder his going. I could not hold the life-destroyer
hard enough—so by a great effort of strength
he made his escape. But he did leave behind   970
his hand, arm and shoulder in a desperate move
to break free with his life. Yet the foe in his frenzy
could not buy relief by paying that price,
for the loathsome marauder will live no longer,
tormented for sins, but his gaping fatal wound   975
has caught him completely in the grip of death,
with unbreakable bonds. Thus he must wait
for the Day of Judgment, smeared with his sins,
to learn his doom from the God of Glory."

  Then the son of Ecgtheow became more silent,   980
no longer boasting of his deeds in battle,
while nobles looked on the sign of his strength
the hand of Grendel high up by the roof,
the fingers of the foe—and each one tipped
with a thick sharp nail, as strong as steel,   985
the claws of the heathen suited for slashing
in horrible slaughter. So each of the heroes
said no sword known to man, no weapon of old,
could do any harm to the bloody battle-hand
of that terrible demon or diminish its power.   990

— XV —

  Then was it ordered that Heorot quickly
be decorated throughout by the many hands there,
both of men and of women, who made ready that
    wine-hall,
the great building for guests. Gold-woven hangings

shone along walls, most wondrous of sights 995
for the assembly of people staring at them in awe.
That bright building had much that was broken
all over inside, yet it still stood fast through its iron bands,
with the door-hinges sprung. Only the roof survived
completely undamaged, when the monstrous creature, 1000
fouled with horrid deeds, sought to make his flight,
without hope of life. There is no easy way,
to flee from one's fate—try as one may—
but every soul-bearer, every child of men,
each dweller on earth, is destined to seek 1005
his appointed place, compelled by necessity,
with his body held fast in its bed of death,
to sleep after feasting. Then was the time fitting
for the son of Healfdene to enter the hall,
for the king wished to join in the festive event. 1010
Never have I heard that a greater host of people
bore themselves better with their giver of treasure.
The glorious gathering sat down on the benches,
to rejoice at the feast, while in the high hall
Hrothgar and Hrothulf,* the kinsmen of those 1015
strong-hearted men, drank many a mead-cup
in great good will. All Heorot throughout
was filled with friends, for treacheries had not
yet been performed by the people of the Danes.
Then Hrothgar gave Beowulf the sword of Healfdene, 1020
and a golden standard as sign of his victory—
a shining battle-banner—with helmet and armor.
Many looked on as they saw the great sword
borne before the hero. As Beowulf partook of the hall-cup,
he need not feel ashamed in front of the warriors 1025
for the splendid gifts that he had been given.

---

*Son of Halga and nephew of Hrothgar.

Never have I heard of many among men
giving four such treasures, adorned with gold,
in more friendly fashion to others on ale-benches.
Round the crown of the helmet was a rim wound
    with wires, 1030
held fast from without, as a fortress for the head,
so a shower of swords, blades sharpened by files,
might not cause severe wounds, when bearing his shield
the warrior must go forth in battle against foes.
Then the protector of earls ordered eight horses 1035
with gold-plated bridles led forth on the floor,
inside the hall. A saddle made with utmost skill,
richly adorned, was set on one of the horses:
that was the war-seat of the high king Hrothgar,
when the son of Healfdene wished to engage 1040
in the play of swords. Never did his prowess
fail in the forefront where the slain fell around him.
And then to Beowulf this defender of the Danes
gave each of the gifts, conferring power
over horses and weapons that were his to enjoy. 1045
Thus the renowned prince manfully paid
for the glory in battle from the people's hoard,
with horses and treasures—so none could find fault
with his generous giving, if speaking the truth.

— XVI —

And then the Danish prince, protector of earls, 1050
gave riches and ancestral treasures to each of the men
there on the mead-bench who made with Beowulf
the voyage over sea. He further ordered that payment
be made in gold for the man whom Grendel
had wickedly killed—and wished to kill more 1055
if he were not prevented by the providence of God

and the bravery of Beowulf. The Creator has ruled
over all humankind, even as he does to this day.
Therefore sound thinking is everywhere best,
the pondering of mind. Many shall live through   1060
the good and the bad who for a long time live
here in the world during these days of strife.
   Then singing and music were mingled together,
performed in the presence of Healfdene's war leader.*
Harp strings were strummed and tales often told   1065
as Hrothgar's scop, entertaining the hall,
was moved to relate, along the mead-bench,
the story of Finn's sons[15] when fighting broke out
and the hero of the Half-Danes, Hnaef of the Scyldings,
was doomed to fall on the Frisian battle field.   1070
   Surely Hildeburh had no reason to honor
the good faith of the Jutes, for she was without guilt
deprived of her dear ones, both son and brother,
in the shield-play: they were fated to fall,
wounded by spears. She was a most mournful woman!   1075
Not at all without cause did this daughter of Hoc
bemoan fate's command when the morning came.
For then she might see under light from the sky
baleful murder of kinsmen, where always before
she had worldly joy. War swept away almost all   1080
the retainers of Finn, except only a few,
so that he could not further engage in fighting
the battle against Hengest, Danish leader after Hnaef,
in that place of slaughter, nor dislodge their survivors
by strength of arms. But peace-terms were settled: 1085
the Jutes would provide other quarters to the Danes,
a hall and high-seat, where they could have power
over half, sharing the rest with the sons of the Jutes;

---

*Hrothgar.

and the son of Folcwalda,* at each day's gift-giving
would bestow honors on the band of Danes,   1090
handing out rings to Hengest, and all his troop,
a great wealth of treasures, plated with gold,
given just as freely as those he gave to Frisians
whom he wished to encourage in the beer-hall.
Then on both sides they arrived at agreement,   1095
firm treaty of peace. Finn swore to Hengest
with inviolable oaths, that he would accord
the Danish survivors the honors determined
by his wise advisors, and that not any man
should break their treaty, by words or by works,   1100
nor through evil contrivance should ever complain,
that since the fall of their king, the Danes now followed
their ring-giver's slayer, for necessity forced them.
If any one of the Frisian men were to call to mind
the murderous feud through foolhardy speech,   1105
then the edge of the sword should settle the matter.
Men prepared for the funeral fire with precious gold
brought up from the hoard. The best of heroes
of the War-Scyldings was placed on the pyre.
On top of the pyre one could easily see   1110
mail stained with blood, golden images of swine,
the iron-hard boar—many brave warriors
dealt death by wounds. Many indeed fell in that slaughter!
Then Hildeburh ordered her son to be placed
fast by Hnaef on the pyre to commit to the flames,   1115
for burning the body, and with him positioned
at his uncle's shoulder. The woman then wailed,
sang out in her grief, as that warrior was raised up.
The greatest of funeral-fires wound up to the heavens,
roaring from the burial mound, while heroes' heads melted, 1120

---

*Finn.

wound-openings burst, and blood sprang forth,
from gashes in the bodies. The greediest of spirits,
flames swallowed all whom war swept away,
both Danes and Jutes, as they departed this life.

— XVII —

Then the warriors went forth to seek out their
    dwellings,   1125
having lost their friends, to look out over Frisia
on their homes and high stronghold. Meanwhile Hengest
dwelled with Finn through the death-stained winter,
without any choice. He thought of his homeland,
though he was unable to sail out on the sea   1130
in his ring-prowed ship—storm surges welled up,
driven by great wind, and winter locked up the waters,
bound fast in the ice—till another year came around,
among dwellings of men, as it does to this day,
forever observing the proper order of seasons,   1135
with wondrous weather. Then winter was gone,
the earth's bosom fair, the Dane eager to leave,
the guest from his exile. Yet he gave much more thought
to vengeance for treachery than he did to a sea-voyage,
how he might bring about a hostile encounter,   1140
since he bore in his mind the sons of the Jutes.
So he did not refuse the rule of custom
when the son of Hunlaf* laid in his lap
a bright shining war-sword, the best of blades—
its edges were already well-known to the Jutes.   1145
Thus did brave-hearted Finn suffer a cruel fate,
struck down in his home, by a death-dealing sword,
when two Danish warriors, Guthlaf and Oslaf,

---

*Danish warrior.

just come back from the sea, complained of the treachery,
blamed Finn for their woes. Such restless spirit   1150
could not be restrained. Then was the hall reddened
with the blood of foes, even as Finn was cut down,
the king in his troop, and the queen taken safely.
The warriors of the Scyldings then bore to their ships
all the house-goods possessed by the lord of that land,   1155
including all the jewelery and gems owned by Finn
that they could find. Then setting forth on the sea,
they carried noble Hildeburh back to her home
among Danish people.

           Thus the lay was performed,
the singer's sad tale. Then revelry sprang up,   1160
a great noise among benches, as bearers of cups served
wine from great vessels. Then Wealhtheow came forth,
crowned with gold circlet, where the two good men sat,
nephew and uncle, who were then still at peace,
each true to the other. And court-spokesman Unferth   1165
sat at the feet of the Danish king. Each one had faith
that he had great courage, though with his kin Unferth lacked
honor in sword-play. Then the queen of the Scyldings spoke:
"Receive this full cup from me, my own dear lord,
great giver of treasures! May you always have joy,   1170
gold-friend of the people, and speak to the Geats
with gracious words, even as a true man should do!
Be generous with these Geats, mindful of gifts
that you have acquired from near and from far.
Men have said that you would wish to have   1175
this hero as your son. Heorot has been cleansed,
the hall bright with rings. You may enjoy many riches
now while you live, and leave to your kinsmen
the people and kingdom, when you must pass on
as destiny decrees. For myself I am sure   1180
that my gracious Hrothulf will hold sway with honor

over the band of young warriors, if you before him
go forth from this world, O Friend of the Scyldings.
I believe that he will bountifully repay
our own sons, if he remembers all the kindnesses   1185
that we bestowed on him to fulfill his wishes,
and conferred on him honors while he was a child."
She then turned to the bench where her sons were seated,
Hrethric and Hrothmund, among young warriors' sons,
youths gathered together. The great hero sat with them,   1190
Beowulf of the Geats, alongside the two brothers.

XVIII —

The cup was borne to Beowulf and offered to him
with words of friendship, and twisted gold presented
with all good will, two ornamented arm-bands,
a mail-coat and rings, and the greatest of neck-rings   1195
as I have heard told, anywhere on the earth.
Nor beneath the heavens have I heard of better
hoard-treasures of heroes, since Hama* carried off
to his bright stronghold the neck-ring of the Brosings,
with jewels in rich settings—fled the battle rage   1200
of Eormenric,† and chose eternal good fortune.
Next Hygelac the Geat, the grandson of Swerting,
had that ring with him on his last expedition,[16]
when under his banner he fought for his treasure,
his spoils from battle. Wyrd swept him away,   1205
when for foolhardy pride he sought his own doom,
in feud against Frisians. That powerful prince
had borne the neck-ring, with its beautiful stones,
over waves to the land where he fell under his shield.

---

*Figure in Northern European legend.
†Famous Gothic king.

Then Franks took possession of the corpse of the king,   1210
the mail round his breast and also that ring,
and warriors of less worth plundered his dead body,
cut down in the battle, where the Geatish warriors
occupied the place of corpses.
                The hall resounded with clamor.
Then Wealhtheow spoke, saluting the warrior band: 1215
"Have joy of this neck-ring, beloved Beowulf,
with good fortune in youth, and use well this mail-shirt
from our people's treasures, and savor prosperity,
win fame through your skill, and give my sons here
your friendly counsel. I shall remember to give you reward. 1220
For what you did here, men will forever
sing songs of praise, both near and far-off,
even as far as the sea flows round the headlands,
the home of the winds. Be ever blessed while you live,
a noble lord. I promise to give liberally to you   1225
from our treasure-hoard. O happy man, I ask of you
that you always act kindly toward my sons!
Here each of the earls is true to all others,
in a spirit of friendship, loyal to their lord.
Thanes are mixing together, in peace as a people,   1230
in fellowship of drinking: they do as I ask."
    She went to her seat. Then warriors drank wine,
the most festive of feasting. They did not know Wyrd,
the grim force of destiny, that would fall upon
many of the earls after evening came and went,   1235
and Hrothgar departed to his own dwelling place,
to rest for the night. A countless number of nobles
protected the hall, as they often had done in the past.
The benches were cleared for bedding and bolsters
to spread over the boards. One of those beer-feasters,   1240
one both lively and doomed, lay down in the hall.
They set by their heads their broad battle-shields,

wood rimmed with bright iron. There on the benches,
hard by each hero, arms were easy to see—
a high battle-helmet, a coat of ringed mail, 1245
a mighty spear shaft. For it was their custom
that they were always made ready for war,
both at home and in war-band, so in either of those
they were equally prepared, if the lord of their people
should have need in distress. That was a brave band. 1250

— XIX —

They sank into sleep. One of those sorely paid
for his rest that night, as had occurred often before,
when Grendel had held sway in that hall of gold,
ruled without right, till he came to his end,
dealt death for his sins. Yet it became known, 1255
widely spoken among men, that still an avenger
lived on after that monster, now a long time
since he met his death. The mother of Grendel,
a female monster, was minded to cause misery.
She was doomed to dwell in some fearsome waters, 1260
streams cold as death, since Cain had committed
the brutal murder of his only brother,
both with the same father. He was fated to wander,
marked for the murder, fleeing the joys of men,
to dwell in the wasteland. From him descended 1265
doomed spirits of old—dread Grendel was one,
that much-hated outlaw, who discovered in Heorot
a warrior on watch, all ready for battle.
There the monster had seized ahold of the hero,
but Beowulf bore in mind his marvelous strength, 1270
a wondrous gift which God had given him,
so he counted on aid from the Almighty,
for help and support. Thus he defeated the demon,

laid low hell's creature, and the wretched one departed,
deprived of joy, to seek out his death-place,   1275
a fallen foe of mankind. And now came his mother,
hungering for men's death, who desired to go
on a sorrowful journey to avenge her slain son.

    She came then to Heorot, where around the hall
the Ring-Danes were sleeping. A reversal of fortune   1280
fell upon those men when the mother of Grendel
penetrated within. The terror of this woman,
her fury in fighting, only seemed any less
when her strength was compared to a weaponed man,
armed with shining sword forged by the smith's hammer,   1285
adorned with blood, slicing through the boar
on an enemy's helmet with its battle-proved edges.
Then all over the hall men took up their sharp swords,
their blades from the benches, and many a broad shield
was heaved up by strong hands. They did not even think   1290
of their stout mail-coats when seized by this terror.
She was in haste, wished to escape that hall,
to save her life, now that she had been seen.
Quickly she laid hold of one of those heroes,
held him fast in her grip, then rushed off to the fen.   1295
That doomed man was the dearest to Hrothgar
of his noble retainers anywhere between the seas,
a strong shield-bearer, whom she slew where he slept,
a widely-famed warrior. Nor was Beowulf there,
but he was earlier assigned another resting-place,   1300
after the giving of treasures to the glorious Geat.
Shouts cried out in Heorot: she had taken the famed hand,
covered with gore, and now grief surged once more,
brought again to their homes. It was not a good bargain
that those on both sides were driven to deal   1305
with the lives of loved ones. Then the wise Danish king,
the hoary old warrior, grew heavy in heart

when he learned his chief thane* was no longer living,
and came to realize his dear friend was dead.
Quickly Beowulf was fetched, a man blessed with victory,   1310
to the king's bed-chamber. At the break of day,
he went with his warriors, a noble champion
among his companions, to where the king waited,
longing to know whether the Almighty would ever
bring about change after this long spell of suffering.   1315
The war-worthy man walked across the floor,
with his band of heroes—the hall-wood resounded—
so that he could address the king of the Danes
with formal words, asking if he had enjoyed
an agreeable night after the evening's feasting.   1320

— XX —

Hrothgar replied, the ruler of the Scyldings:
"Ask not about gladness! Grief is renewed
for the Danish people. Aeschere is dead,
the elder brother of Yrmenlaf the Dane.
Gone is my counselor, my close advisor,   1325
my shoulder-companion when we in warfare
shielded our heads as troops clashed in conflict,
striking boar-helmets. So should a warrior be,
a loyal leader of men, as Aeschere surely was!
Here in Heorot, he was slain by the hand   1330
of a wandering marauder. I know not where
she went from here, exulting in the horrid carcass,
reveling in her feast. Thus she avenged the feud
from your slaughtering her son two nights ago,
in fearsome fighting with your powerful grip,   1335
since he had a long while destroyed and depleted

---

*Aeschere.

the numbers of my people. He perished in battle,
forfeited his life, and now comes another
of the mighty evil-doers to avenge her kinsman,
and she has gone far to reach her revenge,   1340
as many a thane may certainly think,
who grieves for Aeschere, his giver of treasure,
in the pain of heart-sorrow. The hand now lies dead
which ever dealt kindly with all you desired.

    I have heard my people who live in this land,   1345
my own hall-counselors, relate strange stories
that they themselves saw two of such
great march-dwellers holding sway in the moors,
unearthly creatures. One of that couple was,
as far as they clearly might make out,   1350
the likeness of a woman, while the other wretch
walked the ways of exile in the form of a man,
though much more massive than any other human.
From olden days, those who dwelt in those lands
named that one Grendel. They knew not his father,   1355
or whether that father ever had other offspring,
dark-spirited creatures. They lived in a distant land
of desolate wolf-slopes and of windy headlands,
a dangerous marsh-path. A mountain stream there
departs in dark mist far under the rock walls,   1360
an underground flood. It is not far from here,
measured in miles, where the mere stands.
Great trees hang above it, heavy with frost,
woods held fast by roots overshadow the water.
An omen of evil every night may be seen—   1365
flames on that flood. There is no one so wise
that he can determine its bottomless depth.
Though the heath-stepper, a stag with strong horns,
seeking safety in woods was forced into flight,
pressed hard by hounds, it would rather surrender   1370

its life on the bank before jumping in that water
to protect itself. That is no pleasant place!
Towering waves, surge upward on high,
dark under clouds, when the wind whips up
terrible storms, and the sky blackens with gloom   1375
as the heavens wail.

> Our only hope for help
rests with you alone. You have not yet encountered
that place of great peril, where you can find
that creature of sin—seek it if you dare!
I will give you gifts, many ancient treasures,   1380
for your help in this feud, even as I earlier gave
twisted gold rings, when you return a victor."

— XXI —

Beowulf spoke, the son of Ecgtheow:
"Do not grieve, wise warrior! It is better for each man
that he avenge his friend than to mourn him much.   1385
Each of us must accept the end of life
here in this world—so we must work while we can
to earn fame before death. For a warrior it is best
to live on in memory after life has departed.
Arise, protector of the people, let us quickly go   1390
to look for the tracks left by Grendel's kinswoman.
I promise you this: she shall not find shelter,
not in the earth's embrace, nor in mountain woods,
nor the bottom of the sea—go wherever she will!
For today keep patience during all your troubles,   1395
which is what I know to expect of you."
Then up leapt the old ruler, giving thanks to God,
the mighty Lord, for the words this man spoke.

Then Hrothgar's horse was saddled and bridled,
a steed with braided mane. The wise king went forth,   1400

fully equipped, with his war-band marching on foot,
shouldering their shields. The tracks of the enemy
were clear to see along paths through the woods,
going over the ground, heading straight toward
the murky moor, where the mother of Grendel   1405
bore the lifeless corpse of the best of chieftains
who ruled with Hrothgar over their homeland.
The noble band of warriors picked their way
over steep stone-slopes, up a narrow path,
going one-by-one on the unknown way,   1410
by high headlands—home to many monsters.
Hrothgar rode ahead with a few advisors,
from among his wise men, to scout the area,
when he abruptly encountered great mountain-trees,
leaning out over masses of old gray stone,   1415
a wood without joy, overhanging the water
stirred up with blood. Then all the Danes suffered,
their spirits in pain, as grief pierced the nobles,
these friends of the Scyldings, for many a thane
felt comrade-loss when they came upon   1420
the head of Aeschere on the cliff by the mere.
Brave warriors looked on waters roiling with blood,
seething with gore. Time and again, the horn sounded
a song eager for battle, as the war-band rested.
They saw in the water a great swarming of serpents,   1425
strange sea-beasts roaming around the mere,
and water-monsters sprawled on the slopes of the cliffs,
which often in mid-morning set out to hunt prey,
bringing sorrow to many along the sail-road,
these dragons and beasts. They slid from the banks,   1430
bulging with bitter hate, when they heard the call
of the war-horn for battle. A Geatish warrior cut off
      the life,
the warring in waves, of one such monster

with a bow-shot arrow, so that the strong shaft
sank into its heart. Then was it slower in swimming   1435
through seas, as it was seized in the grip of death.
That wondrous wave-roamer was quickly grappled,
with ferocious force, right there in those waters,
by spears tipped with cruel barbs for attacking boars
and dragged onto shore. There men looked on   1440
that horrible strange beast. Then Beowulf put on
his armor for battle, without fear for his life.
His coat of mail, with hard links forged by hand,
broad and well-fashioned, was sufficiently strong
to safeguard his life while searching the waters,   1445
so no battle-clashing might injure his breast,
nor furious foe's grasp might rob him of life.
And a gleaming helmet guarded his head,
for whatever he met at the bottom of the mere,
plunging in surging waters wearing that treasure   1450
with splendid bands encircled, as a smith in old times
had fashioned weapons for war, adorned with wonders,
the likenesses of boars, so that no sword or battle-blade
might ever bite through to bring harm to the hero.
Then to aid him in his time of need, Hrothgar's
    hall-speaker   1455
did not lend the Geat the least powerful of weapons—
a great hilted sword by the name of Hrunting,
which was one of the foremost of ancient treasures,
a blade of iron etched with adders entwined,
made strong by battle-blood. Never had it failed
    any man   1460
whose hands had wielded it in the heat of battle,
daring to go forth on a venture fraught with terrors
in the homeland of foes. Nor was it the first time
the sword was called on to perform deeds of courage.
It seems that strong Unferth, the son of Ecglaf,   1465

did not bear in mind the taunts he had spoken before,
drunken with wine, when he lent this great weapon
to the better sword-warrior. He would not himself dare
to take a chance with his life under the war of the waves,
doing deeds of bravery. Thus he lost lasting fame,　　　　　1470
his reputation for boldness. That was not so for Beowulf,
as he armed himself with war-gear for battle.

— XXII —

Then Beowulf spoke, the son of Ecgtheow:
"Consider now, famous kinsman of Healfdene,
wise prince, and gold-giving friend to the people,　　　　　1475
I am eager for this exploit that we two spoke of—
if in relieving your need I should lose my life,
I ask you ever after to assume the place
of devoted father when I have departed.
May you keep watch over my young warriors,　　　　　1480
my comrades in arms, if in combat I perish.
Also, dear Hrothgar, send on to Hygelac
the trove of treasures that you gave to me.
Thus may the king of the Geats, the kin of Hrethel,
see in that gold, when he stares on the treasures,　　　　　1485
that I met here a great munificent ruler,
a giver of gold rings, and took joy while I could.
And do let Unferth, that widely known warrior,
have the ancient heirloom, the wave-patterned sword,
with its sharp blade. Meanwhile with Hrunting,　　　　　1490
I will seek glory, or death will sweep me away!"
　　　After these words, the prince of the Weder-Geats
hastened away with courage, not waiting at all
for any reply. Roiling waters enveloped
the battle-brave man. Then some time passed　　　　　1495
before he might make out the bottom of the mere.

At once the one who was thirsting for war,
who ruled over these waters a hundred half-years,
grim and blood-greedy, saw that a man
sought from above this world of strange monsters. 1500
She stretched out to attack him, seizing the hero
in horrible grasp, yet she did not do harm
to his sturdy body, for ringed-mail surrounded him,
so that she might not pierce through that protection,
between the locked rings, with her loathsome talons. 1505
The sea-wolf wrestled this prince in ringed-armor,
bore him down to the bottom, to her own hall,
so he could not—though his courage was strong—
wield any weapons. There he was hard-pressed
by strange beasts in the water; many sea-monsters 1510
tore at his mail-shirt with their savage tusks,
pursuing their prey. Then the hero discovered
that he was inside some enemy hall
where he was not threatened by water at all,
nor might he be touched by sudden surgings of flood 1515
because of the hall-roof. He saw light of a fire,
a brilliant gleaming, brightly shining.
    The hero saw clearly the demon of the deep,
the mighty mere-woman. He repaid her fierce attack
with his battle-blade, not holding back his stroke, 1520
so the ring-adorned sword sang out on her head
a war-song greedy for blood. Then the Geat found
that the battle-flasher had lost power to bite,
to slash away life, for the sword-edge failed
the prince in his need. Till now it prevailed 1525
in hand-to-hand fighting, shearing through the helmet
and the mail of a fated man. This was the first time
the great treasure had failed to live up to its fame.
Then Hygelac's kinsman thought only one thought:
not to give up his courage, be mindful of glory. 1530

The angry warrior threw down the patterned weapon,
adorned with art, where it lay on the ground,
strong and steel-edged: he put trust in his strength,
the might of his hand-grip. Thus shall a man do
when he seeks to gain long-lived glory   1535
in furious combat, not caring for his life.
Not flinching from the feud, the prince of the War-Geats
grasped hold of the shoulder of the mother of Grendel,
and bulging with rage, fighting hard in the battle,
he swung her around till she fell on the floor.   1540
Right away after that she repaid his tactic
and crushed him against her in brutal embrace.
She wrestled to throw her spirit-weary foe,
the strongest of warriors, till he slipped and fell down.
She sat on her hall-guest and drew out her dagger,   1545
broad and bright-edged, hoping to avenge her son,
her only offspring. Across his shoulders lay
the woven mail-shirt watching over his life,
guarding against both knife-point and blade.
Then the son of Ecgtheow, stout hero of the Geats,   1550
would have journeyed to death, under wide earth,
except that the battle-shirt, the mail made for war,
provided protection—and the holy God
decreed which was the victor. For the wise lord,
the Ruler of Heaven, decided according to right,   1555
so the hero of the Geats easily got to his feet.

— XXIII —

Then he saw among war-gear a victory-blessed sword,
an old blade made by giants with edges strong and sharp,
the glory of warriors. That was the greatest of weapons,
though its size was so large that no other man   1560
might bear it out to the play of battle—

it was huge and heroic, the work of giants.
The champion for the Danes,* in a dreadful fury,
despairing of life, seized the hilt of the sword,
swung its great blade and angrily struck   1565
so that it dug deep in the neck of the monster,
breaking the bone-rings, slicing all the way through
her body doomed by fate, and she fell dead on the floor.
The sword sweat blood, while the warrior rejoiced.

    The light was gleaming, glowing from within,   1570
as bright as the shining up high in the heavens,
the candle of the sky. The hero searched the hall.
The thane of Hygelac, raging and resolute,
turned by the wall, and heaved up the weapon
high by the hilt. That sword was not useless   1575
to the battle-hardened warrior, and he wished
right then to repay Grendel for the many attacks
which he had delivered against the West-Danes—
far more often than one time only,
when he slew in their sleep Hrothgar's companions,   1580
gorging on fifteen of the folk of the Danes,
as they lay in their beds asleep and unwary,
and bore away with him as many more men,
as gruesome spoils. So the grim champion repaid
him for those horrors, as he saw Grendel lying,   1585
wearied by war, in his last place of rest,
long without life, since his arm was ripped off
in their clash at Heorot. The corpse burst open
when even after death it was struck by the sword,
a vicious battle-blow, and the hero cut off its head.   1590

    The wise warriors with Hrothgar then saw,
as they gazed out over the waters,
that the tossing of the waves grew troubled,

---

*Beowulf.

as blood stained the mere. Gray-haired old men
spoke to each other about the great champion, 1595
saying they had no hope for that hero's return—
that he could come back, triumphant in war,
seeking their famous lord. For the group agreed
that the wolf of the waters* had put him to death.
By mid-afternoon, no man had remained 1600
of the brave Scyldings. The gold-giving king
had departed for home. The Geats sat still,
sick in spirit, and stared at the mere.
They wished to see their war-lord himself,
but had given up hope.
               Then the blade of the mere-sword, 1605
drenched in battle-blood, began to dissolve
into icicles of gore—a great wonder to tell,
that the weapon was melting much like the ice
when the Father loosens the bond of the frost,
unfastens fetters on the waters, wielding power 1610
over seasons and times. That is the true Ruler.
The prince of the Weder-Geats took no
    more treasures
away from that hall, though he saw many more—
except for Grendel's head along with the hilt
of the much-adorned weapon, whose blade had melted, 1615
the wave-marked iron burning, for the blood was so hot
from the poisonous demon who had died in that place.
Then the one who survived the deadly struggle,
the fall of his foes, swam up through the water,
and waves tossing together throughout that expanse 1620
were entirely cleansed, when the alien creature
took leave of his life-days and this transitory world.
    The chief of the sea-men then swam to the shore,

---

*Kenning for a water monster, which, in this case, is Grendel's mother.

a brave-hearted hero. He rejoiced in the booty,
the mighty burden he brought from beneath the waters. 1625
The bold war-band rushed toward him, all in a crowd,
giving thanks to God, and shouting with joy
that they now could see their prince safe and sound.
Then off of that hero the helmet and mail-shirt
were quickly taken. The mere grew calm, 1630
the water under clouds, stained with slaughter-blood.
Then they went forth along the foot-paths,
joyful in mood, marching along dirt-trails,
on the well-known way. Bold noble warriors
carried Grendel's head down from the headlands, 1635
a long hard labor for each of the bearers,
all high-spirited men. No fewer than four
were needed to hold up the head of Grendel
on the shaft of a spear, going to the gold-hall,
till presently they came, brave and battle-bold, 1640
all fourteen Geats going together as they marched
to Hrothgar's great hall. The valiant chieftain
strode among his men through the plain by the mead-hall.
The leader of these loyal thanes, renowned for deeds,
honored with fame as a battle-brave hero, 1645
went into the hall to salute King Hrothgar.
The Geats bore Grendel's head by the hair
out onto the floor where the Danes were drinking—
a terror to those nobles, and Wealhtheow too,
was that awesome spectacle, for all looking on. 1650

— XXIV —

Then Beowulf spoke, the son of Ecgtheow:
"Hail, son of Healfdene, King of the Scyldings,
gladly have we brought you spoils from the sea,
as a token of glory for you to gaze on here.

I barely survived the battle under water,   1655
to return still alive, having done brave deeds
under great stress. The deadly struggle at the start
would have ended, if God had not watched over me.
I was powerless to prove my strength with Hrunting,
in the fearsome fighting, though the weapon was worthy.   1660
Yet the Ruler over men then granted to me
to see a wondrous weapon hanging on the wall,
a mighty old sword—as God has often guided
one without help from friends—so I heaved it up.
Then I slew in the struggle, when I saw my chance,   1665
the guards of that dwelling. And the blade burned up
on the patterned sword, as blood sprang forth,
the hottest of battle-gore. Then I carried the hilt
away from those fiends, having fittingly avenged
the wicked deeds that brought death to the Danes.   1670
I promise you now, that you may sleep safely
here in Heorot with your band of warriors,
and all of the thanes from among your people,
both youths and veterans. You need not feel fear,
O King of the Danes, that your deadly enemies   1675
will tear life from your friends, as you feared till now."
Then was the golden hilt, the ancient work of giants,
given over to the hand of the old warrior,
the hoary battle-chief: the work of wonder-smiths
passed into possession of the lord of the Danes   1680
after the death of the demons, and the hostile creature
the enemy of God, guilty of murder,
gave up life in this world along with his mother.
It came into the power of the best of princes,
of those who hold sway in this world between seas,   1685
giving rich gifts in the realm of the Danes.

    Then Hrothgar spoke, as he looked on the hilt,
the old heirloom, engraved with its tale of origins

of ancient strife, when the surging of the sea
rushed in a flood, sweeping to slaughter   1690
the kinship of giants, of creatures estranged
from the eternal Lord—through the whelming waters
the Ruler dealt them their final retribution.
The name was made known, clearly marked out,
in the shapes of runes* shining with gold,   1695
on the sword-guards, for whom the smith first
wrought that best of weapons, with twisted grip,
and patterns of serpents. Thus the wise king spoke,
the son of Healfdene—and all fell silent—
"Truly a man may announce, who acts according to right   1700
among his own people, as an old guardian of the land,
recalling past deeds, that this noble hero here
was born the best in history. Your fame is renowned
wherever men journey, my dear friend Beowulf,
among all the peoples. You hold power with balance,   1705
with wisdom of mind. Now I shall fulfill our friendship
as we earlier agreed. And you shall bring
peace to your people for a long time to come,
a source of strength to the heroes. Not so was Heremod†
to the sons of Ecgwela, the honorable Scyldings.   1710
He did not bring them success, but slaughter instead
and destruction for the people of the Danes.
Carried away with rage, he killed table-companions,
his close loyal comrades, till this ill-famed prince
journeyed all alone from the world of men's joys.   1715
Although mighty God had given him power,
the pleasures of strength, and raised him in ruling
over all other men—yet there grew in his heart

---

*Characters in ancient Scandinavian and Germanic alphabets; they were used on
monuments, as artistic decorations, and in sacred rituals.
†He is an example of a bad king, whose story is told beginning with line 901.

a bloodthirsty breast-hoard. He gave out no treasures,
to earn glory among Danes, but he dwelt without joy,   1720
forced to suffer the rewards of the strife that he caused,
the long-lasting evil to his people. Then learn from this,
understand proper virtue! I have told you this tale
from the wisdom of many winters. For it is wondrous to say
how the mighty God, through magnanimous spirit,   1725
gives out as gifts to the kin of men their wisdom,
lands and rulership. He is lord of all things.
At times God allows the thoughts of a man
of a famous family to turn to what he loves,
giving such a man joy in his homeland,   1730
while holding sway over his stronghold of men.
God renders him rulership over such regions,
a wide-spread kingdom, yet the man cannot see,
because of his folly, an end to his fortune.
He lives his life in the joy of feasting, not at all   1735
hindered by sickness or age, his spirit not darkened
by sorrow over evil, nor does strife from enemies
display sword-hatred, but fulfilling his desires
the world goes on—he knows nothing worse.

— XXV —

"Until arrogant pride sprouts in his spirit   1740
and grows large within, while the guardian of his soul
falls off to sleep—a sleep far too sound,
beset by cares, with a killer quite near
who wickedly shoots an arrow from his bow.
Then hit in the breast under his helmet   1745
by the piercing arrow, he cannot protect himself
against the sinister commands of the evil spirit.
His long-held treasures he thinks too little,

and grasps them grimly, not proudly giving
rings graced with gold, forgetting and neglecting   1750
that the Ruler of Glory, God had formerly given him
prosperous destiny, his great portion of honors.
Thereafter in the end, it ever comes to pass
that man's short-lived flesh proves itself frail,
fated to fall. Then another comes to power,   1755
who gives out great gifts without any care,
sharing with the nobles without fear of loss.
Defend yourself against malice, dear Beowulf,
the best of men, and choose the better course,
everlasting profits. Do not foster pride,   1760
glorious warrior! The great fame of your might
lasts but a little while. Then soon enough
will sickness or the sword deprive you of strength—
or the grasp of flames, or the surging flood,
or the slashing blade, or the flight of a spear,   1765
or horrid old age. The brightness of your eyes
will diminish and grow dark, and then even you,
great hero among men, will go down in defeat to death.

    Thus have I ruled the Ring-Danes under the heavens
for fifty winters, waging war to protect them   1770
against many peoples throughout this middle-earth,
with spears and swords, so I did not consider myself
to have any enemy remaining under the sky's expanse.
But hear! My homeland suffered reversal of fortune,
of grief following happiness, after Grendel the invader   1775
became my monstrous enemy for many years.
Without any break, I bore that oppression,
with much sorrow in spirit. May the Creator be thanked,
the eternal Lord, that I survived with life,
so that I may see with my own eyes   1780
that sword-bloodied head after the long struggle!

Go now to your seat, have joy in celebrating
the honors from battle, for between us two
many riches will be shared when morning comes."
    In gladness of spirit, the Geat then went   1785
to seek out his seat, as the wise king directed.
Then once more as before, a feast was made ready,
for heroes famed for courage, sitting in the hall
for this occasion. The shadows of dusk deepened,
spreading darkness over all. Seasoned warriors rose up,   1790
as their hoary-haired king, old ruler of the Scyldings,
wished to seek his bed. Well pleased was the Geat,
the famed shield-warrior, to find his own rest.
Then a hall thane showed the way to the warrior,
come from a far land, and weary from his venture.   1795
The thane ministered to the needs of the man
with all due courtesy, such as in those days
seafaring warriors were supposed to receive.
    The great-hearted hero took his rest. The hall rose up,
broad and gold-adorned. The guest slept within,   1800
until the black raven with blithe spirit announced
the joy of the heavens.* Then brightness hastened,
[daylight after darkness.] The warriors moved quickly,
as the nobles were eager to embark on the journey
back to their people. The brave-hearted visitor   1805
wished to seek out his ship far from that hall.
    Then battle-brave Beowulf ordered that Hrunting
be brought to Unferth, for him to take back the sword,
the beloved blade, and thanked him for that gift.
The Geat said he thought the sword a good war-friend,   1810
bold in battle, and said that he found no fault
in the edge of the blade. That was a high-minded man!

---

*Kenning for the sun.

Then eager to depart, the Geats were all dressed,
ready in war-gear. Their prince who had won honor
among the Danes, the brave hero in battle,   1815
went to Hrothgar's high-seat, and greeted the king.

— XXVI —

Beowulf spoke, the son of Ecgtheow:
"Now we seafarers, come from far off,
wish to say we desire your leave to seek out
our own King Hygelac. We have been welcomed here   1820
most graciously. You have hosted us well.
If I can do anything in this wide world
to earn from you greater heart's affection,
ruler over men, than I have already performed
of works of war, I shall stand ready.   1825
If I should hear, over the stretch of the sea,
that neighboring nations threaten you with war,
as enemy peoples have done in the past,
I shall bring to your aid thousands of war-thanes,
an army of heroes. I know that Hygelac,   1830
the king of the Geats, protector of his people,
though young in years, will support me in this
with words and deeds. Thus I will honor you well,
and bring into battle a forest of spears,
to support you with strength, when you have need of men. 1835
If some time your son Hrethric should decide to come
to the court of the Geats, he could count on finding
many friends there. It is truly fitting to visit
faraway countries for a man of real worth."
Then Hrothgar spoke, gave reply to the Geat: 1840
"The Ruler of Wisdom has sent well-formed words
into your head. Never till now have I heard

such mature speaking by a man so young.
You are strong in might, prudent in spirit,
wise in word-smithing. I fully expect   1845
that if it should happen, that the shaft of a spear,
sword-grim battle, sickness or blade of iron
swept away Hrethel's son, your dear lord,
the people's protector—and you still have life—
that the Sea-Geats could not seek anywhere   1850
to find a better choice for their own king,
hoard-guardian of heroes, if you would rule
the kingdom of your kin. I admire your spirit
more and more as time passes, dear Beowulf.
You have brought it about, that both our peoples,   1855
the nations of Sea-Geats and of Spear-Danes,
shall share in the peace, and put strife to rest—
the malicious evil they endured before—
while I wield power over the wide kingdom,
treasures will be shared, and many a man will greet   1860
another with gifts over the gannet's bath.*
The ring-prowed ship shall bring over the seas
tokens of mutual affection. I know my countrymen
forever remain firm with both friend and foe,
unswervingly faithful to ancient tradition."   1865
      Then the safeguard of nobles, the son of Healfdene,
gave him gifts in the hall, twelve treasures in all.
Hrothgar bade him seek safety among his dear people,
to come quickly back to them with precious gifts.
Then the king of noble lineage, the lord of the Scyldings,   1870
kissed the best of thanes, Beowulf the Geat,
and clasped his neck, while tears dropped down
from the hoary-haired ruler. Old and very wise,
he might expect one of two things, but especially one—

---

*Kenning for the sea; a gannet is a large water bird, similar to a heron or pelican.

that after this day they would not see one another,   1875
as brave men meeting together. Beowulf was to him so dear
that he could not control the surgings in his breast,
but in his heart the bonds of spirit held fast,
and he kept secret the longing that burned in his blood
for the dear man to stay. Then Beowulf strode away,   1880
over grassy turf, a gold-proud warrior,
exulting in treasure. The sea-going ship
awaited its master, riding on anchor.
While sailing over waves, the gifts of Hrothgar
would often be praised. For he was a prince   1885
in every way blameless, until conquering old age,
as with many others, stole from him the joys of strength.

— XXVII —

Then the company of brave young comrades
came to the sea. They wore coats of mail,
woven with interlocked rings. The coastguard watched   1890
the approach of this band, as he had done before.
He did not insult them by greeting these guests
from the rim of the cliff, but rode down toward them,
proclaiming these shining warriors returning to their ship
would be most welcome to the people of the Weders.   1895
Then on the beach the curved wide boat
was loaded with war-gear, the ring-prowed ship
filled with horses and treasures. The mast towered
high over the hoard of riches given out by Hrothgar.
To the guardian of the boat Beowulf gave a sword,   1900
bound round with gold, so later on the mead-bench
the man was more honored for holding this treasure,
an ancient heirloom. Then Beowulf mounted the boat,
to drive through deep waters, leaving the Danish land.
There by the mast was a sheet of sea-garment,   1905

a sail held fast by a rope. The ship's planks creaked;
the wind over waters did not hinder the wave-floater
from steering its course. The sea-vessel plunged on,
its neck spraying foam, floating over the flood,
the tightly bound prow pitching over the streams—   1910
till the sailors could see the high cliffs of the Geats,
the well-known headlands, and the ship shot forward,
buffeted by winds, to land up on the beach.
At once the harbor-guard, who had eagerly gazed,
looking far out over the ocean for a very long time,   1915
expecting these comrades, stood ready by the sea.
He steadied on the sand the wide-bosomed ship,
made fast by anchor-ropes, so the might of the waves
could not carry away the fine wooden craft.
Then Beowulf gave orders to bring the noble treasures,   1920
precious adornments and plated gold, for it was not far
for them to seek their great giver of gifts,
Hygelac son of Hrethel, where he dwelt at home,
surrounded by retainers, nearby the sea-wall.

    The building was splendid, the bold king sitting   1925
in the high hall, along with Hygd, his very young queen,
who was wise and accomplished, though very few winters
had this daughter of Haereth spent dwelling there,
within the stronghold. She was not mean in spirit,
nor sparing in giving gifts of rich treasures   1930
to the Geatish folk—far different from Modthryth,
herself a high queen, who committed outrages.
There was no man among the close comrades
so brave as to dare to look on her by day,
with eyes upon her, except her own husband,   1935
but he could count himself destined for deadly bonds
artfully woven. Soon after that he was seized,
held by strong hand-grips for the doom of the sword,
so the bright patterned blade would settle the matter,

displaying deadly evil. That is no way for a queen   1940
to exercise power, though she may have no equals—
she should be a peace-weaver,[17] not fake a pretext
to take away life from a loyal retainer.
So the kinsman of Hemming* put a stop to that.
Men drinking ale told a different tale,   1945
that she produced less distress among the people,
far fewer hostilities, after she was given in marriage,
adorned with gold and of goodly lineage,
to the young chieftain, following her father's advice,
and sailed over the yellow waves to take her seat   1950
in Offa's hall. Afterward she made excellent use
of her queenly throne, became famous for goodness
as long as her life-span was ordered by fate.
She held noble love for the chieftain of heroes,
who of all mankind, as I have heard told,   1955
was the very best living between the seas
of all the nations. For Offa was famed
as a spear-skilled man, and widely honored
in gift-giving and war, ruling with wisdom
his own native land. Then Offa fathered Eomer,   1960
champion of heroes and kinsman of Hemming,
grandson of Garmund, skillful in battle.

— XXVIII —

Then Beowulf the bold went with his war-band,
striding over the sand to the plain by the sea,
along the wide shore. The world-candle[†] shone,   1965
the sun hastening from the south. Marching together,
they quickened their pace, toward the protector of nobles,

---

*Offa, a king of the Continental Angles.
†Kenning for the sun.

the slayer of Ongentheow,* inside the stronghold,
the young war-king, who had proved his worth
giving rings to retainers. There King Hygelac   1970
was right away told of Beowulf's arrival—
that back to his home, the king's guardian of comrades,
his shield-companion, had come full of life,
unharmed from sword-sport, to greet him in court.
Space was quickly cleared, within the wide hall,   1975
as the king directed, to welcome the foot-warriors.

     Then with the king sat the one who survived
the deadly fighting, kinsman opposite kinsman,
as the ruler of men gave ceremonial greeting,
with earnest words. The queenly daughter of Haereth[†]   1980
went round the high hall with vessels of mead,
showed love to the people, sharing the drinking cup
among the heroes. Then Hygelac began,
pressed by curiosity, politely to question
his companion sitting there in the high hall   1985
about the adventures of the Sea-Geats:
"How did you do on your voyage, dear Beowulf,
after all of a sudden you resolved to go off,
to seek deadly combat far over salt waters,
hand-fighting at Heorot? Have you for Hrothgar,   1990
the prince of renown, somewhat remedied
his widely-known woes? Worried over this venture,
I have seethed with sorrows, yet did not trust the chances
of my beloved friend. For long I entreated you
not to take on in battle that deadly terror,   1995
but let the South-Danes settle their own scores,

----

*Hygelac, who did not actually kill Ongentheow himself, but who led the force
that did.
†Hygd.

in their war with Grendel.[18] I give thanks to God
that I may now see you back, safe and sound."
    Beowulf spoke, son of Ecgtheow:
"The truth is not hidden, King Hygelac,   2000
among many men, concerning the great meeting
of Grendel and me in the time we two tested
each other in battle, in the place he brought sorrow,
never-ending miseries, to so many of the men
of the Victory-Scyldings. Yet I won vengeance,   2005
so no kinsmen of Grendel can have reason to boast,
anywhere over the earth, about our night-clashing—
no matter who lives longest of that loathsome race,
enveloped in evil. When first there, I went
to the ring-hall to hold counsel with Hrothgar.   2010
As soon as he knew what my heart was set on,
the famous king, the kinsman of Healfdene,
assigned me a seat beside his own sons.
The company was spirited; never have I seen,
under heaven's arch, more joy in mead-drinking   2015
among friends in the hall. At times the famed queen,
peace-bringer to the people, circled around the hall,
urging on the young revelers. Often she gave rings
to some of the men, before she went to her seat.
At times Hrothgar's daughter herself took the ale-cup 2020
to each of the earls in the war-band of veterans,
and I heard the men sitting together in the hall
call her Freawaru, as she passed the studded cup
to each of the heroes. She has been promised as bride,
gold-adorned and youthful, to the gracious son of Froda.* 2025
The king of the Scyldings, protector of his people,

---

*Ingeld, king of the Heathobards.

arranged terms for the union, considered it advisable
that he could settle the conflicts of deadly feuds,
through marriage of his daughter. Yet seldom does it
    happen
that the spear stays at rest, for even a short while,   2030
after a man has been slain—though the bride be splendid!
    Then may the Heathobard prince be provoked,
and each of the thanes from among his people,
when he goes with his wife into the hall,
that her Danish attendants are entertained nobly   2035
and richly adorned with ancient heirlooms,
Heathobard treasures, made hard and patterned,
that were theirs while they might wield those weapons—

— XXIX–XXX —

till they led their own comrades, with themselves as well,
down to destruction in the shield-play of battle.   2040
Then at the beer-drinking, an old spear-warrior will speak,
seeing a Heathobard sword on one of the Danes,
and remembering the slaughter—his spirit made grim—
in this sad mood, he begins to put to the test
a young Heathobard hero, awakening in his heart   2045
the fury of war through uttering these words:
'My dear comrade, can you recognize that sword,
the fine old blade, that your father bore
into the battle, with his helmet strapped on
for the last time, when he was struck down by Danes,   2050
the powerful Scyldings, who controlled the killing-place
when our Withergyld* fell, in the slaughter of heroes?
Now in this hall some young son of those murderers
swaggers out on the floor, gloating in our arms,

---

*Heathobard warrior.

boasting of the carnage, and bearing the old sword, 2055
the one that you by right ought to possess.'
Thus he tempts the young warrior every time he can,
with stinging words, until the moment arrives
when the offending thane of the queen is cut down,
bloodied by the bite of the blade, forfeiting his life 2060
for his father's deeds. His Heathobard foe
escapes with his life, since he knows the land well.
Then the oaths sworn by earls on both sides
will be broken. After that deadly rage wells up
against Ingeld, and after new troubles arise 2065
his love for his wife begins to become cooler.
Thus I would not count on the firm friendship
of the Heathobard people, nor on peace made by
    marriage,
without deceit toward Danes.
                    I shall now return to speak
more about Grendel, so that you, giver of treasures, 2070
may fully know how we finally concluded
the hand-fight of heroes. When the gem of the heavens*
had gone gliding beyond earth, the monster came raging,
a gruesome night-terror, seeking to take us by storm
where we were yet unharmed, holding the hall. 2075
The onslaught turned out to be fatal for Hondscio,
fated for grim death, the very first of the victims,
a well-armed warrior. Grendel the man-eater
tore with his teeth the famous hall-thane,
gulping the dear man's body all the way down. 2080
Still the bloody-toothed killer, intent on more slaying,
did not wish to depart from the gold-adorned hall
without more bodies to bear away in his grip,
but he would pit his renowned might against me,

---

*Kenning for the sun.

grasping with hands. He held hanging down   2085
a wondrous wide bag, skillfully closed with clasps—
it was cleverly designed for its deadly use,
with the craft of the devil, out of dragon skins.
This wild savage worker came up with the plan
to shove me inside, though I had done no evil,   2090
with many others as well. But that might not be,
for in a towering fury I stood upright.
It would take long to recount how I then repaid
that enemy of people for each of his evils,
while the deeds I performed there, my dear prince,   2095
brought honor to your people. Yet Grendel got away,
to enjoy what he could of his little time left,
though his strong right hand remained behind
as a trophy in Heorot, while he wretchedly went forth,
mournful in mood, to sink down to the mere-bottom.   2100
For that deadly fight, the friend of the Scyldings
gave me as reward many gold-plated treasures,
a great store of riches, after morning arrived,
and we had set ourselves down to feast in the hall.
There was singing amid the general good cheer,   2105
and an old Scylding told tales from far-back lore.
At times a battle-brave warrior took up the harp,
striking joy from the strings, relating a story
both tragic and true; then the great-hearted king
told a wondrous tale in traditional fashion.   2110
Sometimes an old warrior, stooping with age,
started to make speeches to the band of youths
about boldness in battle. His heart surged within,
as he brought to mind his wisdom of many winters.
Thus we passed the whole day in the hall,   2115
taking our pleasure, till the night once again
came over the men. Then quickly after that
the mother of Grendel prepared revenge for her grief,

making sorrowful journey. Death had seized her son
in war with the Weders. This monstrous woman   2120
got vengeance for her kin by killing a Danish hero
boldly in his bed—her victim was Aeschere,
a wise old counselor who went forth from this life.
Nor the next morning might the Danish people
lay their dead friend on a funeral pyre   2125
for the flames to consume the fallen body
of the beloved man. For she carried off the corpse,
in a fiendish embrace, under the mountain-stream.
That was the most grievous of griefs for Hrothgar,
which the prince of his people had to endure.   2130
Then the Danish king, sorrowing in spirit,
begged me on your behalf to perform heroic deeds,
to dare mortal danger in the tumult of waters,
to chance all for glory, promising me great gifts.
Then I sought down through surging waters   2135
the well-known grim guardian at the bottom of the mere.
For a time we two locked in hand-to-hand combat;
then the waters welled with blood, as I cut off the head
of Grendel's mother, with a mighty sword-blade,
down in that war-hall—and after such danger,   2140
I departed still living, for I was not yet fated to die.
But the king of the nobles, the kinsman of Healfdene,
afterward rewarded me with a great many riches.

— XXXI —

   Thus the Danish king acted according to custom,
and so not at all did I lack for rewards,   2145
rich payment for heroism, but the son of Healfdene
gave me wealth to take home, to dispose as I wished.
I bring all this to you, the king of brave warriors,
giving it with gladness. For you are the source

of every favor, and I have few near-kinsmen 2150
except for you, Hygelac, my uncle and king."
    Then Beowulf had men bring the banner with
    boar-symbol,
the helmet worn high for battle, the gray mail-shirt,
the patterned war-sword—while giving formal speech:
"Hrothgar the wise prince gave me this war-dress, 2155
asked me to assure you, with a certain few words,
that he wishes you to know of his good will toward you.
He said that Heorogar, former King of the Danes,
prince of the Scyldings, long possessed this armor.
Yet he would not pass on this breast-protection 2160
to battle-bold Hearoweard, the king's own son,
even though he was loyal. Make use of it well!"
I have heard that four horses, all fast and alike,
with colors of bay, yellow shading to brown,
followed those gifts. Beowulf bestowed on him both, 2165
the horses and treasures. Such should a kinsman do—
not braid a net of malice for other men,
with secret craft, nor prepare to send a comrade
down to his death. The nephew of Hygelac
was ever loyal and true, in the toughest fighting, 2170
and each one was mindful for the other's good.
I heard that Beowulf gave Queen Hygd a neck-ring,
wondrously ornamented, given him by Wealhtheow,
now his gift to royal Hygd, with three graceful horses,
bearing shining saddles. Ever after receiving the ring, 2175
her breast was adorned with the bright jewel.
    Thus the son of Ecgtheow showed himself to be brave,
a man famed for fighting, with heroic deeds,
living ever for glory. He never slew hearth-companions,
in drunken fury, nor did he have a frenzied spirit, 2180
but the brave-battle man guarded the generous gift,
given him by God, of the greatest strength

of all mankind. For many years he had been scorned
as the Geatish warriors considered him worthless,
nor did the lord of the Weders wish to do him honor   2185
among the young men seated on the mead-bench:
they thought him to be slow and slothful,
not qualified as a war-lord.[19] Yet a turn-around came
for every act of disdain toward the glorious hero.

    Then the protector of nobles, the battle-brave king,   2190
ordered the heirloom of Hrethel, adorned with gold,
to be brought in the hall. No sword was the least better,
a greater treasure among Geats, during that time.
Hygelac laid the sword on the lap of Beowulf,
and handed over to him seven thousand hides of land,*   2195
with a hall and a prince's seat. Those two together,
in that country, lawfully held large territories,
their lands by ancestral right, but Hygelac's was larger,
in that broad kingdom, because his rank was higher.

    Afterwards it happened, a long time later,   2200
in deafening battles, when Hygelac lay dead,
and his son Heardred was slain by war-swords,
struck down under the defense of his shield,
when the battle-bold warriors, the Heatho-Scylfingas,†
hunted him down with his war-band of heroes,   2205
attacking hard against this nephew of Hereric‡—
then Beowulf became ruler of the broad kingdom,
the realm of the Geats, which he ruled over well
for fifty long winters—that was a wise king,
old protector of his people—until the time when,   2210
in the dark of night, a dragon began to swell with power,
which had been holding watch over a hoard on the heath,

---

*A hide was a measure of land of sufficient size to support one family.
†Literally, "Battle-Scylfings," pronounced "Shilfings"; the reference is to the Swedes.
‡Heardred, king of the Geats after Hygelac, who is succeeded by Beowulf.

a high burial mound, where a path lay beneath,
unknown to men. Yet one man found the path,
making his way nearby, and he went inside   2215
to the heathen hoard, seizing a cup with his hand,
a large ornamented treasure. Though it had been tricked,
while it was sleeping, the dragon made no secret
of the plunder by the thief. The neighboring people
soon found out the terror of its fury.   2220

— XXXII —

The thief did not break into the dragon-hoard,
desecrating the creature's home, according to design,
but out of sore distress. This slave of some master
was forced to flee the beating of hostile blows,
in need of a shelter, and compounding his shame,   2225
he invaded the mound. [Then when he saw the monster,
this unwelcome guest stood still in horror.
Yet the wretched man made his way forth,
sought safety from the wrath of the dragon,
slipping away from a sudden attack,   2230
stealing][20] the precious cup. Many such riches,
treasures from ancient times, lay in that earth-house,
an immense legacy of a noble nation,
a precious hoard, which some man had hidden
in days long gone by, considering with care   2235
that place of concealment. Death seized all his people,
in time gone by, and this lone man was the only
      one living
from the band of warriors, still walking their lands,
a lone watchman mourning friends, expecting the
      same fate,
that for only a short moment might he enjoy the riches 2240
long-held by his people. The barrow was prepared,

standing on a plain, near the surging of sea-waves,
newly built on the ness, artfully made hard to enter.
The guardian of ring-gifts bore inside the barrow
a mass of ancient treasures, adorned with gold, 2245
worthy of a hoard, and said these few words:
"Hold safely, O Earth, what the heroes cannot,
the wealth of our nobles! Of course, men of worth
first found it on you. War-death swept away,
in malicious slaughter, every one of the men 2250
of my own people, who had once known hall-joy,
before leaving this life. I have no one to wield a sword,
or polish the precious vessel, plated with gold,
the drinking cup for feasting, now that comrades
    are gone.
The high bold helmet, skillfully wrought with gold, 2255
will lose its gold plating, while those assigned to polish
the war-masks have long departed in the sleep of death.
So also the mail-coat, which came through fierce fighting,
the sharp biting of blades, in the clashing of shields,
decays like the warrior. Nor may the ringing mail 2260
travel far and wide on campaigns with the war-chief,
protecting the sides of the hero. Nor is there joy of
    the harp,
gladness of the wood-strings; nor does the good hawk
swing through the hall; nor does the swift horse
tramp through the stronghold. Terrible death has indeed 2265
sent forth from this world many nations of men!"[21]
Thus sad in spirit, he sang his lay of sorrow,
the last one to live, unhappily moving
through day and night, till death's surging power
reached into his heart. Then the old night-raider, 2270
a smooth-skinned dragon that burned in the dark,
flying through night skies enveloped in flames,
seeking out barrows, took joy in the hoard-treasure

which it found wide open. Greatly was it feared
by the folk of that land. It was forced by its nature   2275
to seek the hoard in the earth, where it stood old in winters,
guarding heathen gold—yet from that got no good.
    Thus for three hundred winters that evil enemy
held sway over the hoard-hall there in the earth,
huge and powerful, till one man provoked anger,   2280
rousing it to rage. The run-away man bore the treasure
to his own master, pleading for peace with his lord
and safe haven as well. Thus was the hoard plundered,
its store of gold-treasures decreased, and the plea granted
to the miserable man. And the lord looked upon   2285
the ancient work of long-gone men for the first time.
Then the dragon rose from sleep, and discord was renewed.
It moved swiftly over stones, till the bold-hearted creature
found its enemy's footprint, where the man had stepped,
sneaking with stealth, near the head of the dragon.   2290
Just so, may a man who is not fated to fall
pass securely to safety, from woe and exile,
who has the Almighty's favor! The hoard-guard searched,
anxiously about the ground, hoping to find the man
who did such a wrong while the dragon was asleep.   2295
In a heated mood, and a troubled mind, it often circled
the outside of the barrow, but there was not any man
in that wasteland—yet it now yearned for war,
hoped for battle-joy. At times it turned toward the mound,
still seeking the treasure-cup, but it soon found   2300
that one of mankind had gotten into the gold,
the heap of riches. Then the hoard-guard waited,
tortured in mind, till evening arrived.
The barrow's protector was bulging with rage,
the dragon desiring to avenge with flames   2305
the dear drinking vessel. When day had departed,
as the creature wished, no longer would it wait

on the wall of the barrow, but went forth with fire,
eagerly blazing. That was the beginning of terror
for folk in that land, as it soon ended in sorrow   2310
for their great giver of treasures.

— XXXIII —

Then the monster began to spew forth flames,
burning bright dwellings; light from fires shot up,
while the men watched in horror. For the hateful
    night-flyer
did not wish to leave any one of them living.   2315
The dragon's war could be widely seen,
its fearful cruelty observed near and far—
how this war-ravager both hated and humbled
the people of the Geats. Then the dragon darted back
to the secret hall of its hoard, before it was day.   2320
After the monster enveloped all who lived in that land,
in a blazing inferno, it trusted for safety in the barrow,
its fighting force and the wall. That hope was deceived.
Then was the terror made known to Beowulf,
swiftly and surely, that his very own home,   2325
the best of buildings, the gift-scat of the Geats,
was melting in waves of flame. That was heart-sorrow,
the greatest of griefs, for the good ruler.
The wise king considered that he bitterly offended
the Almighty Lord, the Eternal Chieftain,   2330
by breaking ancient law.[22] His breast within
welled with dark thoughts, as were not usual for him.
The fire-dragon had destroyed with flames
the stronghold of the people, the land bordering the sea,
the fortress of the nation. For that the war-king,   2335
the prince of the Weders, planned terrible vengeance.
The champion of warriors, the chief of the nobles,

ordered a wondrous war-shield to be made for him,
entirely of iron, since he knew for certain
that a wooden shield could provide no protection,   2340
when fire attacked wood. The long-famous king
had lived to see the end of his life-days,
in this transitory world, along with the dragon,
though it had long held the wealth of the hoard.
Then did Beowulf, the ruler of riches, refuse to seek   2345
the far-flying terror with a band of warriors,
a large fighting force, for he was not filled with dread,
nor did he think much of the monster's war-skill,
its power and boldness, because always till now
he had survived every danger, braving many battles,   2350
the crashing of combat—since the time long ago,
when blessed with victory, he cleansed Hrothgar's hall,
and with his mighty grip, killed the kin of Grendel,
that loathsome race.
                    Nor was that the least
of deadly hand-combats, when men slew Hygelac,   2355
the king of the Geats, the kinsman of Hrethel,
lord and friend to his folk, during a raid in Frisia,
in the storm of battle, beaten down by blades,
with swords drinking blood. Beowulf returned from there
by his own skill, swimming over the sea,   2360
having captured alone thirty coats of armor,
battle-gear of enemies, when he attained the sea-side.[23]
None of the Hetware,* who bore against him
shields of linden-wood in the fighting on foot
could boast after battle, since only a few   2365
escaped that war-hero to seek their own homes!
The son of Ecgtheow, alone and wretched,
swam back to his people across the broad sea.

---

*Franks who fought against the Geats in the Frisian raid.

Queen Hygd offered him the kingdom and its hoard,
treasures and the king's throne, for she did not trust   2370
that her son could wield power to protect the nation
against foreign foes, now that Hygelac lay dead.
Yet those grieving people could in no way prevail
upon that noble hero, in any of their assemblies,
that he would become the lord over Heardred,   2375
or choose to hold a position of kingly power.
Thus Beowulf gave the prince full support with the folk,
friendly counsel and honor, till he was old enough
to rule the Weder-Geats. Yet Ohtere's sons from over
    the sea
sought Heardred's protection, while fleeing a feud,   2380
for raising arms against Onela, their father's brother,
the lord of the Scylfings, the best of sea-rulers,
of all those in Sweden who gave out rich gifts,
a famous king. Thus Hygelac's son Heardred
reached his limit of life-days, when for giving them shelter   2385
he took deadly wounds from the slashing of swords.
Then the Swedish king Onela, the son of Ongentheow,
left to seek his own home, after laying Heardred low,
making way for Beowulf to hold the high throne,
to wield power over his people. That was a good king.[24]   2390

— XXXIV —

In later days, Beowulf bore vengeance in mind
for Heardred's fall, and he became a friend to Eadgils,
who was totally helpless, and supported Ohtere's son
in fighting across the wide sea, with a war-band,
giving warriors and weapons. He thus avenged Heardred,   2395
in a bitter campaign, taking life from King Onela.[25]
And so he survived, the son of Ecgtheow,
every one of the dangers of brutal battles,

his tests of courage, till at last the day came
when he would be forced to fight with the dragon.   2400
Then the ruler of the Geats, swelling with rage,
went in a troop of twelve to observe the dragon.
By then he had heard how the feud arose,
a scourge to men, since by the betrayer's hand
the priceless cup came into his possession.   2405
With them there, as the thirteenth man,
was the one who had caused all of this conflict,
the wretched fugitive, who in misery was forced
to show the way. He went against his will
to the site where he saw the underground hall,   2410
the barrow under earth, close by the surging sea,
where wave wrestled wave. The mound inside was full
of treasures and wire ornaments. The terrible guardian,
well-prepared for fighting, possessed those gold-riches,
old under earth. That would be no easy bargain   2415
to be obtained by any one of the race of men.
The battle-hardened king sat down on the headland,
their gold-giving friend wishing good fortune
to his hearth-companions. His spirit was sad,
restless and ready for death—his fate drawing near,   2420
which would seek out the old warrior
to find the hoard of his soul, and to sever the tie
of his life with his body. Not for long after that
was the spirit of the war-chief wound up in the flesh.
    Then Beowulf spoke, the son of Ecgtheow: 2425
"While a young man, I survived many battle-storms,
the waging of war. I now remember all that.
I was seven winters old when the ruler of treasures,
the lord and friend of the folk, took me from my father.
Hrethel the king kept me and fostered me,   2430
gave me gold treasure and feasting, mindful of kinship,
and I was not loved any less while he lived,

a boy in the stronghold, than any of his sons,
Herebeald and Haethcyn, or my own lord Hygelac.
For the eldest son a death-bed was spread   2435
by a dreadful deed that was caused by a kinsman,
when his brother Haethcyn drew his horned-bow,
and let fly an arrow that missed the mark,
striking down the prince, killing the kinsman,
one brother the other, with the bloody shaft.   2440
No compensation could be paid for the wrongful death,
no consolation in mind. The prince had to lose his life
without hope of atonement, nor being avenged.*

    So also is it mournful for an aged man
to be forced to suffer when his young son swings   2445
high on the gallows. Then he sings a lay for his lament,
a sorrowful song, while his son hangs dead,
a treat for the raven, yet for all his age and wisdom,
he may not provide any help to his poor son.
Always in mornings, there will come into his mind   2450
the image of his son's awful end. He does not even care
to wait in his stronghold for another son's birth,
one to be his heir, since his first son departed,
forced by fate to suffer a terrible death.
He looks with great sorrow upon his son's home,   2455
a desolate wine-hall, where only winds dwell,
having lost all joy—the horsemen sleep in death,
the heroes in graves, nor does the harp sound
its happy notes in the hall, as it used to do.[26]

---

*The father cannot take vengeance on his own son for accidentally killing his
other son.

— XXXV —

He goes to his bed singing a lay full of sadness,   2460
his song for his son. His lands and his home now seem
too large for himself alone.
                              So also did King Hrethel,
protector of the Geats, store grief in his heart
after Herebeald's killing, for he could in no way
seek for revenge on the slayer of his son,   2465
nor could he let loose hatred toward Haethcyn
for his hateful deed, though he was not dear to the king.
In the midst of this misery which quite overcame him,
Hrethel gave up men's joy and chose God's light,
leaving his sons the lands and towns of his people,   2470
as a good man does, when he departed this life.
        Then feuding and strife between Swedes and Geats
broke out in bitterness of each nation to the other,
over the wide waters, after Hrethel passed away.
The sons of Ongentheow the Swede[27] proved themselves   2475
brave and strong in battle, and did not wish to maintain
friendship across the seas, but they often fought
with death-dealing malice around Hreosnabeorh.*
My kinsmen and friends took a fearful vengeance
for that feud and that crime, as is known far and wide,   2480
though one warrior paid for winning with his life,
a hard bargain indeed. For in that fateful battle
Haethcyn was killed, the king of the Geats.
I have heard it told, that in the morning Hygelac
avenged his brother. The killer was slain by the sword,   2485
the old Swede Ongentheow, who was seeking for Eofor.
The helmet was sheared of this aged Scylfing,

---

*Hill in Geatland.

who fell down pale as death. Not forgetting the feud,
the hand did not hold back in striking that blow.

    In battle I paid Hygelac* back for the treasures   2490
he had bestowed on me, wielding my bright sword,
as my fate would have it. He gave me fine lands,
an ancestral home. There was no need for him
to seek among Gifthas,† or among Spear-Danes,
or in the kingdom of the Swedes, to search for   2495
a lesser warrior than myself to reward with riches.
Whenever fighting on foot, I was always in front,
alone before him, and so will I do battle,
as long as life lasts, and this sword survives,
which has at all times stood steadfastly by me.   2500
In front of our forces, I killed Daeghrefn,‡
the Frankish champion, in hand-to-hand fighting—
he could not bring back to the king of the Frisians
any breast-adornments worn by our warriors,
but he fell in battle, the guardian of the banner,   2505
a hero in strength. Yet the sword did not slay him,
but my battle-grip crushed his bone-house,
stilled the beating of his heart. Now with a blade,
with my sword in hand, I have to fight for the hoard."

    Then Beowulf spoke, gave his boasting-speech   2510
for the last time: "I have lived through many battles
while in the strength of my youth, yet still I wish,
as old protector of my people, to seek out this fight,
to win great glory, if the man-slaying monster
will come out of his cave to meet me in battle."   2515
Then he saluted the company, his beloved comrades,
the courageous heroes with helmets strapped on,

---

*Now king of the Geats, after the death of Haethcyn, his brother.
†An East Germanic people.
‡Killed by Beowulf in a bear-hug.

for the last time: "I would not wish to bear a sword,
a weapon against the dragon, if I knew another way
to fulfill my boast, to grapple with this beast,   2520
as I did against Grendel a long time ago.
But here I will face a foe breathing fire,
blazing and venomous—so I must do battle
under shield and mail-shirt. Yet I will not yield a step
to the hoard's guardian, so we will test by the barrow's wall 2525
which one of us two wins the favor of fortune,
as the Creator decides for all. Since my courage is strong,
I need not make a boasting-speech against the war-flyer.
I bid each of you to wait near by the barrow,
protected by mail-coats, proud warriors in arms,   2530
to see which of us two can better survive wounds
after the tumult of battle. This task is not yours,
nor is it fitting for any other man, except me alone,
to measure strength against the monster,
in heroic war-deeds. With courage I will win   2535
a reward of gold treasures, or your king will be torn
away from his people in a frightful slaughter."

   Then the renowned warrior rose up with his shield,
bold under his helmet, bearing his battle-coat
under the stone-cliffs, and trusting in the strength   2540
of himself alone. Such is not cowardly conduct!
He who survived many dangerous struggles,
swords crashing together, strong in his manhood,
when warriors on foot clashed madly with weapons,
now saw a stone arch, with flames streaming out,   2545
bursting forth from the barrow. The waves of that stream
surged with battle-fires, so no one could come near,
or live through the passage leading down to the hoard,
because of the flames of the dragon's breath.
Then the king of the Weder-Geats, filled with fury,   2550
let a loud shout burst forth from his breast;

his strong heart storming, his voice roared out,
his battle-cry ringing in the ancient stone barrow.
The hoard-guard then was seething in hatred
at those threatening words. This was no time   2555
for seeking a truce. First from the stone-hall
came the monster's breath, eager for burning,
a searing thrust. The earth thundered.
Hard by the barrow, the brave lord of the Geats
swung up his shield against the stranger's terror,   2560
as the creature coiled, making itself ready
to launch its attack. The bold battle-king
brought forth his sword, a strong ancient blade,
its edges not blunted. Each of those enemies,
intent on killing, inspired fear in the other.   2565
Stern in spirit, the ruler of his comrades
stood with his shield, waiting in his war-gear,
as the dragon quickly coiled itself together.
Then balled up and burning, the dragon slithered forth,
speeding to its fate. The shield served less well,   2570
and for a shorter while, than hero had hoped
to protect life and body of the famous prince.
For the first time in his life, there on that day,
he had to wield war-strength without Wyrd assigning
him victory in battle. The bold lord of the Geats,   2575
raising the treasured sword high in his hand,
struck the many-colored monster, but the blade failed
when it hit the bone, biting far less deeply
than the king of his people, pressed hard by dangers,
needed for the kill. Then was the keeper of the barrow,   2580
after that battle-blow, fierce in its fury,
spewing out deadly fires, the flames of war
sweeping the ground. The gold-friend of the Geats
might not boast of battle-triumph, for the naked blade
had faltered in the struggle, the famous old iron   2585

failing its mission. It was no easy move
for Ecgtheow's kinsman, the widely-famed king,
to give up ground to the hated enemy.
He would be forced to depart, against his will,
from his home and land, as each man must,   2590
leaving this fleeting life.
                    It was then not long
that the two fierce fighters again joined battle.
The hoard-guard took heart, its breast again swelling
with breathing forth fire, as the people's king Beowulf
was pinned down and suffering, surrounded by flames.   2595
Not then did his comrades, the kinsmen of nobles,
close ranks around him, draw a line of defense,
a brave fighting force. But they fled to the woods,
where they saved their lives. Yet in one of them surged
a feeling of remorse, for he well remembered   2600
the bonds of loyalty, as he considered his kinship.

— XXXVI —

He was called Wiglaf, son of Weohstan,*
a valued shield-warrior, a man of the Scylfings,
a kinsman of Aelfere. He saw his lord suffer
the blast of the heat burning under his helmet.   2605
He did not forget the favor he received in times past,
the prosperous place among the Waegmundings,†
and each ancestral right he held from his father.
He could not hold back, but his hand heaved the shield,
the yellow linden-wood; he seized the time-honored
    sword‡   2610

---

*The last surviving kinsman of Beowulf.
†Family to which Wiglaf and Beowulf belong.
‡Description of the passage of the sword from Eanmund to Weohstan to Wiglaf.

that was one of the trophies taken from Eanmund,
the son of Ohtere. Weohstan had slain him,
a friendless exile, in a fateful battle,
with the blade of his sword, and carried to his kinsmen
the shining helmet, the ringed shirt of mail,   2615
the gigantic old sword—gifts given him by Onela,[28]
the battle-armor of Eanmund, his brother's son,
with ready war-gear. Nor did Onela speak afterward
concerning their feud, though Weohstan killed his kin.
The victor held those treasures for many half-years,   2620
the shining sword and shirt of mail, until his own son
could perform bold deeds, as his father had before.
When in his old age, he left from this life,
among the people of the Geats, Weohstan gave Wiglaf
a countless collection of arms. And now was the first time   2625
for the brave young warrior to withstand such fury,
the storm of battle, standing beside his beloved lord.
His spirit did not waver, nor would his father's weapon
fail in the fighting—as the dragon would discover
when they both had come together in battle.   2630
    First Wiglaf spoke, said to his comrades
many words of truth, while he mourned in spirit:
"I remember the day, when we were drinking mead,
and we pledged loyalty to our prince
in the beer-hall, while he was giving us gifts,   2635
that if ever he were driven to such distress as this,
we would repay him for our war-gear,
our helmets and strong swords. So for this venture
by his own will he chose us, from all his war-band,
thought us worthy of glory, and gave me these treasures,   2640
for he considered us steadfast spear-warriors,
bold in our helmets—though our brave lord
had planned to perform, all by himself,
this great work of courage, as protector of his people,

since he among men had done the most daring of deeds, 2645
winning the greatest glory. Now has the day come
that our dear lord is in desperate need of the strength
of good men in battle. Let us then go to him,
provide help to our war-prince, while there is still
fierce fire-terror! God knows this about me, 2650
that I would much rather that my own body
be embraced by the flames standing with my gold-giver.
It does not seem to me brave that we bear our shields
back to our home, unless we first use our strength
to protect the life of the prince of the Weders, 2655
and destroy the dragon. For I know that Beowulf,
with his past deeds of glory, does not deserve
to suffer such affliction, by himself among the Geats,
and sink down in defeat. Together we shall share
the same sword and helmet, the mail-coat and armor." 2660
Then Wiglaf strode through the smoke of death,
with his helmet to help his lord, and spoke few words:
"Beloved Beowulf, give this fight your best effort.
As you said in your youth, in days long ago,
you would never allow your fame to fade away, 2665
while you still lived. So now, steadfast leader,
renowned for great deeds, shall you defend your life
with all your strength. I will support you."
　　After he spoke, the huge serpent came raging,
the death-dealing terror striking forth once again, 2670
surging with flames, seeking to attack its hated foes,
the much-loathed men. Waves of fire swept Wiglaf's shield,
burned it up to its boss, nor might the mail-coat
provide needed protection to the young warrior,
but the youth fought on bravely, nonetheless, 2675
under his kinsman's shield, when his own was consumed,
in the storm of fire. Then once more the famed war-king
was mindful of glory, and with mighty strength,

pressed hard by the evil foe, swung his battle-sword,
so it stuck in the dragon's head. Yet Naegling shattered,   2680
Beowulf's great blade, the ancient gray iron,
failed in the fighting. It was not given to him
that he might get help in that hard-fought battle
from the edge of the sword—for his hand was too strong,
so he over-taxed every sword, as I have heard told,   2685
with the power of his swing, when he bore into battle
a wondrously hard weapon. He got nothing from that!

    Then for the third time, the threatening monster,
the frightful fire-dragon, mindful of their feud,
rushed on the famed ruler when he saw an opening,   2690
seething and battle-grim, surrounding his neck
with fierce sharp fangs, digging into his flesh
to drain life from his body, as the blood streamed out.

— XXXVII —

    When the prince of the people had greatest need,
I have heard that his comrade displayed great courage,   2695
great skill and boldness, as befit his nature.
Brave Wiglaf did not strike at the head of the beast,
but his hand was burned in helping his kinsman,
striking the creature somewhat lower down,
so the warrior's sword, gleaming with gold,   2700
plunged into the dragon, and the deadly flames
began to die down. Then once more the king
gained control of himself, and gripped his short sword,*
sharpened for battle, that he wore at his waist,
and the people's protector sliced through the serpent.   2705
They had felled their foe, bravely taking its life,
and the two had together brought down the dragon,

---

*Worn at the hip, this was considered to be the weapon of last resort.

as noble kinsmen. Thus should a thane always act
in time of need! That was the last of the triumphs
that the prince accomplished through powerful deeds,   2710
of his works in this world. For soon the wound
that the dragon had dealt him during the struggle
began to burn and to swell. And then he felt
the murderous poison from the monster's fangs
well up in his breast. Then the bold king went   2715
to sit himself down by the side of the barrow,
thinking deep thoughts, looking on that work of giants—
how stone arches inside that ancient earth-hall
were held firmly in place supported by pillars.
And then the thane, who proved loyal without limits,   2720
took water in his hands to wash away the blood
from his famous prince, his lord and friend,
who was weary from battle, and unfastened his helmet.

    Then Beowulf spoke, wounded as he was,
and wretchedly suffering. He clearly realized   2725
that he had gone through the days given to him,
his time of joy on earth. His long life was hastening
to depart, and death was extremely close by—
"Now I would wish to give my war-gear
to my son, if fortune had so favored me   2730
that I would be able to leave arms to an heir,
my own offspring. I have ruled over my people
for fifty winters, and there is no folk-king
of any of the neighboring nations around us
who ever dared to attack me with allies,   2735
threatening with terror. In the time I was given,
I lived in my own land, ruling my people well,
never turning to treachery, or swearing to oaths
contrary to right. In all this I take comfort and joy
when now I am stricken with death-dealing wounds.   2740

The Ruler over mankind has no reason to charge me
with murdering kinsmen, when my life leaves,
departs from my body. Now, dear Wiglaf,
make haste to look upon the hoard in the mound,
under old gray stone, since the dragon lies dead,   2745
sleeps from sore wounds, stripped of the treasure.
Go quickly now, so I may readily gaze
on the long-held riches, look on the gold treasures,
the bright-beaded gems, and thus I may more peacefully,
for winning this wealth, pass on from this life,   2750
leaving behind my people, whom I long have ruled."

— XXXVIII —

I have heard it said that after Beowulf spoke,
the son of Weohstan quickly obeyed his wounded lord,
weakened from battle, and went under the barrow's roof,
wearing his mail-coat, the war-shirt woven with rings.   2755
Then the brave young kinsman, exulting in conquest,
saw many precious jewels as he passed by the seat,
glittering gold lying around on the ground,
a wonder on the wall, and the den of the dragon,
old flyer by night. Standing nearby were drinking cups,   2760
vessels from former times, with no one to furbish them,
their ornaments long gone. Here was many a helmet,
ancient and rusty, and piles of arm-rings,
twisted with skill. Such a wealth of treasures,
gold lying in the ground, even if it is hidden,   2765
may easily seduce any man anywhere!
He also saw on high, hanging over the hoard,
a standard sewn with gold, artfully hand-woven
with the greatest of skill. From it came a glow,
so he might make out what lay on the floor,   2770

and inspect all the treasures. For no trace of the dragon
remained by the hoard, since the sword swept him off.
    And I have heard it told that the hoard was plundered,
the barrow built by giants, when the man alone
took as he wished, wrapped his arms around riches,   2775
stealing cups and dishes, and also the standard,
the brightest of banners. The sword of Beowulf,
that blade of iron, had earlier injured
the one who protected those precious treasures
for a long time, waging terror with flames,   2780
fighting for the hoard with fierce searing heat,
in the midnight skies, till he met violent death.
    Wiglaf the retainer made haste to return,
urged on by the treasures. The true-spirited man
wished to know whether he would find   2785
the prince of the Weders still living though weak,
in the same place where he had left his lord.
Bearing treasures from the barrow, he found Beowulf,
his beloved king, all covered with blood,
near his limit of life-days. He began to splash water   2790
to revive the war-hero, till the vanguard of his words
broke free from his breast-hoard, and the king spoke,
the old man in his suffering, gazing on the gold:
"I wish to give thanks, speaking such words as I may,
to the almighty Ruler, the King crowned with glory,   2795
the eternal Lord, for these riches I look on
here by the barrow, that I have been blessed to acquire
for my dear people, before the time of my passing.
Since I have traded my old life for these treasures,
long held in the hoard, now you must provide for   2800
the care of the people. For I cannot abide here longer.
Order the battle-famed men to build up a mound,
after the funeral pyre, splendid over the sea,
that shall serve as memorial for my people,

towering high on the headland of Hronesness,* 2805
so that seafaring men may in seasons to come
call it Beowulf's Barrow, as they drive their ships
through the darkness of the deep, having come from afar."
Then the bold-spirited ruler removed from his neck
a golden circlet, and gave it to his loyal thane, 2810
the young spear-warrior—also his gold-gleaming helmet,
ring and coat of mail, commanding him to use them well:
"You are the last man left of all our kin,
the Waegmunding people. Wyrd has swept away
all my family, according to their fates, 2815
all those nobles still in their strength. Now I must follow."
That was the last word the old war-king spoke,
from the spirit in his breast, before he sought the pyre,
the surging of flames, and then his soul traveled,
forth from his breast, to the fame of the righteous. 2820

— XXXIX —

Then sorrow came over the youthful kinsman,
as he looked down in grief, and saw on the ground
the one he loved best at the end of his life,
after wretched suffering. His slayer lay dead also,
the terrible earth-dragon, his life torn away, 2825
in a violent death. The dragon in its coils
no longer held power over the hoard of rings,
since the blades of iron, hard and battle-sharp
from the smith's hammer, severed it from life,
and the monstrous wide-flyer, stilled by its wounds, 2830
was hurled to the ground near the hall of the hoard.
No longer was it seen to be soaring aloft,

---

*Literally, "whale's ness" (a "ness" is a cape or headland); a headland on the coast of
Geatland.

mounting up high in the midnight skies,
reveling in riches, but it fell to the earth
through the war-chief's work in hand-combat.　　　2835
Truly, as I have heard told, few men of might
who lived in that land have enjoyed success,
however daring they were in dangerous deeds,
rushing to battle against that poisonous breath,
or reaching in hands to take from the ring-hall,　　　2840
if they found awake that fearsome guardian,
on watch in the barrow. Yet with his death
Beowulf had paid the price for the many treasures,
for both he and the dragon found a bitter end
to this fleeting life. Then it was not long　　　2845
till those fearful of fighting gave up the woods,
cowardly traitors, ten altogether,
not daring to defy the monster with spears,
proving disloyal to their lord in his need.
They approached in their shame, bearing their shields,　　　2850
their weapons for war, where the old king lay,
while looking at Wiglaf. He sat there weary,
the brave fighter on foot, near his lord's shoulders,
tried to wake him with water, but without success.
He did not have the power to hold life in the prince,　　　2855
here on this earth, though he earnestly wished it,
nor in any way change the will of the Almighty.
For the decree of God ever governs the deeds
of every man, even as it still does today.
Then was it easy for cowards who lost courage　　　2860
to get a stern speech from the young hero.
So Wiglaf spoke, the son of Weohstan,
sorrowing in spirit, with contempt for those comrades:
"Listen to what truth an honest man may tell,
that the very ruler, who gave you rich gifts,　　　2865
the war-gear you wear, now standing beside him—

when often the prince offered those on the ale-bench,
sitting around in the hall, both helmet and mail-coat,
as gifts to his thanes, and so great was their splendor
as he could find, from near and from far— 2870
that he had totally wasted those gifts of war-gear,
given how you behaved when battle came on him.
The king of our people had no cause to boast
of his comrades in fighting. Yet God granted him,
the Ruler of victories, that he himself gain vengeance, 2875
alone with his sword, when he had need of strength.
I could do little to protect his life,
giving support in the battle, yet still I began,
well beyond my power, to provide help to my kinsman.
When I struck with my sword the evil enemy, 2880
it gradually grew weaker, and the fire less fiercely
surged from its mouth. Too few men formed around
to defend the prince, when this distress was upon him.
Now the giving of treasures and gold-adorned swords,
and all joy for your kin in your much-loved land, 2885
will come to a halt. Every one of your kindred
will be made to move on, with the rights to his land
stripped away, when war-chieftains from afar
hear the tale told of your flight from your lord,
that deed without glory. Death is better 2890
for all noble men, than a life of shame!"

— XL —

Then he directed a man to report these deeds
up in the camp over the cliff, where the warriors sat,
in mournful mood, the whole morning long,
shields at their shoulders, expecting one of two things— 2895
either their dear leader's death, or his coming back
once more. The messenger who rode up the headland

kept little back of the news of the battle,
but he told the tale truthfully to all the warriors:
"Now the giver of gifts to the people of the Weders,   2900
the lord of the Geats, lies fast on his death-bed,
his place of slaughter, through the serpent's evil.
And likewise beside him lies that death-dealer,
slain by the hip-knife, for Beowulf's sword
could not cut fatal wounds, in any way,   2905
into the monster. There beside Beowulf,
Wiglaf remains sitting, the son of Weohstan,
one warrior over the other who is now without life,
on guard at the head, holding sorrowful watch,
over both friend and foe. Now may our people   2910
expect a time of war, when the fall of our king
is related far and wide, and cannot be concealed
from Franks and Frisians. Harsh strife with the Hugas*
was caused when Hygelac came with ship-warriors,
launching his raid in the land of the Frisians,   2915
where the Hetware† attacked him with ferocious force,
and overpowered the Geats with greater strength,
so the king in his mail-coat had to give way,
and fell among his fighting men. No riches did the king
give to his bold warriors. Ever since that battle,   2920
the Merovingian king‡ has denied us friendship
        and favor.
        Nor would I predict any peace or good will
from the Swedes, since it was known far and wide
that their old king Ongentheow had stolen the life
of Hrethel's son Haethcyn, nearby Ravenswood,²⁹   2925
when the people of the Geats, in over-reaching pride,

---

*A Frankish people.
†Another Frankish people.
‡King of the Franks.

first sought to strike back at the War-Scylfings.*
Quickly the Swedes' king, the father of Ohtere,
terrible in his age, swung his sword in reply,
killing the Geats' sea-king,† and rescuing his old wife,   2930
a captive of the Geats, bereft of her gold,
the mother of both Onela and Ohtere.
Then Ongentheow followed his deadly foes,
until with great difficulty they got away
into Ravenswood, though now with no ruler.   2935
Then with his veterans he set up a siege
round the wound-weary survivors, often promising
woes to those wretched warriors all night long,
saying he in the morning would slash some of them
with hard-edged swords, and hang others from trees   2940
for the sport of birds. But relief was brought
to the desperate Geats, as daylight first broke,
and they heard the sounds from the horn and trumpet
of their own Hygelac, with that heroic leader
following that blaring with a band of warriors.   2945

— XLI —

Then a gory trail left by Swedes and Geats,
from the storm of killing, could be seen from afar,
how the fury of their fighting boiled with blood.
The bold Swedish king then went with his kinsmen,
old and much-saddened, to seek his stronghold;   2950
noble Ongentheow turned to leave the battle behind.
For he had heard of Hygelac's fighting strength,
the proud man's war-skill, and could not be confident
that he would be able to stave off the seamen,

---

*The Swedes.
†Haethcyn.

to hold the hoard safely, with children and wife,   2955
against these sea-warriors. So the old king turned away,
standing behind the earth-wall. Then the men of the Swedes
were pressed in pursuit, when the standard of Hygelac
completely ran over the refuge of their stronghold,
as the Geatish warriors broke through their walls.   2960
Then blades of swords forced the gray-haired Swede
to stay and stand fast there by the rampart,
so this king of his people had to submit
to the sentence of Eofer alone. He was struck
with the weapon of Wulf, son of Wonred,*   2965
so blood from that blow sprang forth from his veins,
from under his hair. Still he felt no fear,
this aged Scylfing, but struck back with his blade—
far worse in reply than the fierce blow he received—
when the king of his people turned to face him.   2970
Nor was the strong son of Wonred then able
to strike a blow back to answer the old man,
who had cut through the helmet on Wulf's head,
so that stained with blood, the Geat had to give ground,
and then fell to earth—not yet fated to die,   2975
but held on to his life, though horribly wounded.
Then Eofer, the hardy thane of Hygelac,
where his brother lay low, swung his broad sword,
a weapon forged by giants, over the king's board-wall,†
to split his huge helmet. Then the king sank down,   2980
protector of the people, overpowered by death.
Then many comrades bound the wounds of the brother,
quickly raised him up and gave him some room
so they could take control over this killing field.
At once Eofer stripped his fallen foe's body,   2985

---

*Geatish warrior, brother of Eofer.
†Kenning for a shield, which was commonly made of linden wood.

took the iron mail-coat off from Ongentheow,
with his hard-sharp sword and his helmet together,
and bore the hoary king's arms to his own Hygelac,
who gladly took them and gave him fair promise
of rewards among their folk, and that was fulfilled.   2990
The lord of the Geats, Hrethel's son Hygelac,
when he returned to his home, repaid that battle-storm,
giving hugely great treasures to Eofer and Wulf:
to each the cost of a hundred thousand coins
in land and locked rings—no man in middle-earth   2995
could slight that reward to the hard-fighting heroes.
Then as a pledge of good will, he gave to Eofer
his only daughter, to bring honor to his home.
       Such is the source of the feud and hostility,
deadly hatred among men, for which I foresee   3000
the people of the Swedes to come seeking us,
after they have heard it told that our own dear lord
has lost his life, who up to now has protected
our hoard and kingdom against those who hate us,
after the fall of heroes,* bold men bearing shields,   3005
winning the good of the nation, doing noble deeds,
always and ever. Now let us make haste,
so we may look in that place on the people's king,
and carry our ruler, who gave us rich rings,
in procession to the funeral pyre. Not only one thing   3010
shall be burned with the brave man, but all of the hoard,
with its countless gold, purchased at fearful price,
that now at the last he paid with his life
for the precious rings. Then will the fire roar,
embracing all in its flames. Not any of the nobles   3015
will take off treasures as tokens, nor any fair woman
wear around her neck a ring of gold as adornment,

---

*In the defeat of the Geats in the Frisian raid.

but all shall continue to grieve, bereft of gold,
more than once forced to walk in a foreign land,
now that their war-leader has left behind laughter,   3020
all mirth and hall-joy. And so shall the spear,
many times in morning-cold, be clutched in the hand,
heaved up on high, nor will the music of the harp
wake up the warriors, but then the dark raven,
eager to feed on fallen warriors, will speak much,   3025
telling the eagle of his pleasure in eating,
when he with the wolf both feasted on corpses."[30]

    Thus the bold messenger told his bitter tale,
relating his story, not speaking without truth
about the past or the future. The war-band all arose,   3030
and went stricken with sorrow under Earnaness,
their eyes welling with tears, to go see the wonder.
They would find there on the sand, his spirit departed,
lying on his last bed, the one who gave them rings
in days gone by. The good ruler had passed on   3035
in his final day, when the famed war-king,
the prince of the Weders, died a wondrous death.
Yet first they saw a far more strange creature,
the loathsome serpent lying on the opposite side
of that same place. The fierce fire-dragon,   3040
many-colored and fearsome, was scorched with flames.
Stretched out, it reached fifty foot-measures,
lying at full length. It had once taken night-joy
flying through the air, and then drifting down
to seek out its den; but now bound by death,   3045
it had enjoyed its last earth-cavern.
By the dragon stood precious cups and pitchers,
with plates lying around, and priceless swords
eaten through by rust, as if they had remained
there in the earth's bosom, for a thousand winters.   3050
Moreover, that massive hoard of heirlooms,

the gold of men of yore, was held by a chanted charm,
so that none of the race of men might reach
into that hall of rings, unless God himself,
the true King of victories—who has all men in his
    keeping— 3055
grants a person the power to open up the hoard,
a grant given by God to whichever man he thinks worthy.

— XLII —

    Thus was it seen that the dragon failed to succeed
in its effort to hide the hoard under that cliff,
against lawful right. That guardian first had fatally
    wounded 3060
the matchless hero, but for starting that feud the monster
received cruel vengeance. It is ever a question
where a warrior famed for courage may reach the end
of his appointed life-days, when he may no longer
sit down in the mead-hall surrounded by kinsmen. 3065
So it was for Beowulf, when he sought the barrow's guard
in a contest of battle-skills. He himself could not know
how his parting from this world would come about.
Thus the famed princes who placed treasures there
had formally declared, that until doomsday, 3070
any person who would plunder the hoard
would be guilty of sins, trapped in temples of idols,
held fast by hell's chains, tormented by terrors—
unless he had already acknowledged more fully
the power of God alone to give treasures.[31] 3075
    Wiglaf then spoke, the son of Weohstan:
"Often many a warrior, for the sake of one man,
must endure misery, as has happened to us.
Nor might we have persuaded our own dear prince,
the protector of the kingdom, by any of our counsel, 3080

that he not meet in battle the guardian of the gold,
but to let the creature lie where long he had been,
watching over that dwelling till the world's end.
But he held to his high destiny. The hoard is now open,
so grimly won: that fate was too grievous   3085
that pressed the lord of our people to come to this place.
I have been inside that barrow, and looked over all
the treasures in that hall, where the way was made clear,
though no welcome permitted my passage inside,
there under the earth-wall. In haste I took handfuls,   3090
as much as I could carry of a mighty burden,
of the treasures of the hoard, and bore them out here,
for my king to see. He was then still alive,
conscious and clear-headed. The old man then spoke
many things in his sorrow, and said for me to greet you,   3095
bidding you to build, to honor your lord's deeds,
a high barrow on the place of his funeral pyre,
great and glorious, as he was among men
the warrior most famous around the wide world,
during the time he took joy in the kingdom's riches.   3100
Let us now hasten, to look one more time,
to seek out the store of artfully made jewels,
that wonder by the wall. I will show the way,
guide you close so you may gaze on those riches,
the rings and precious gold. Let the bier be prepared,   3105
quickly made ready, when we come out of the hoard,
and then bear away our beloved chieftain,
our dear king and comrade, where he will long remain
in the protection of the all-powerful Ruler."

The son of Weohstan, the battle-brave warrior,   3110
directed that orders be given to many of the men
who held their own halls, that they should bring wood,
from their lands far away, for their king's funeral pyre,
where the good lord now lay: "Now shall the fire devour,

with swelling dark flames, the dear chieftain of warriors, 3115
who has often survived through showers of iron,
when a storm of arrows, urged on by great strength,
shot over the shield-wall, shafts doing their duty,
flying true with their feathers, to direct their sharp heads."
Then after this speech, the wise son of Weohstan 3120
called forth from the band of the king's own thanes
a group of seven together, the best of spear-warriors,
and went with that seven under the enemy's ceiling,
as a band of fighting men. One bore in his hand
a torch for a light, leading the way for the others. 3125
There was then little need to draw lots to decide
who would plunder the hoard, since without its protector,
they could see all the riches still held in that hall,
all wasting away. And little did any of them mourn
that they might quickly carry out from that place, 3130
the priceless treasures. Then they pushed the dragon,
the terrible serpent, over the cliff, to be seized by waves,
as the greedy hoard-guard was embraced by the sea.
Then a wagon was loaded with twisted gold treasure,
countless riches of all kinds, and the noble prince, 3135
the hoary old warrior, was borne to Hronesness.

— XLIII —

Then the people of the Geats prepared for him
a funeral pyre in that place, of no small size,
hung round with helmets, shields for battle,
and shining mail-shirts, to fulfill his request. 3140
Then the lamenting warriors laid in the center
the widely renowned prince, their beloved ruler.
The warriors awakened the greatest of funeral fires
on the high barrow, and the wood-smoke swirled up,
black above the flames, the roaring of the blaze 3145

mingled with weeping—wind-surges ebbed—
till the heat from the fire burst the bone-house,
breaking into the breast. Unhappy in spirit,
the men sadly mourned the death of their lord.
So also an old woman, her hair loose and waving,*   3150
sang in her sorrow a song of lament
for Beowulf's passing, repeating her prophecy
that she feared invading armies of bitter foes,
a great many slaughters, the terror of war-troops,
humiliation and captivity. Heaven swallowed the smoke.   3155
     Then on the cliff, the Weders set to work,
building a barrow that was both high and broad,
which could be seen from afar by seafaring men.
Ten days later, they finished making the monument
to their battle-bold lord, with a wall built around   3160
the remains from the fire, the finest construction
that the very wisest of men might design.
They brought to the barrow precious rings and jewels,
all such adornments as the brave-spirited men
had earlier taken away from the enemy's hoard.   3165
They left the treasures of earls in the earth for keeping,
the gold in the ground, where yet it still lies,
as fruitless to men now, as it formerly was.
Then men bold in battle, the sons of chieftains,
all twelve together, rode around the barrow,   3170
expressing their grief, and lamenting their lord,
with words wrought in song, a dirge for the dead.
They sang of his valor, and his deeds of great strength,
with all their power praising the hero—as it is fitting
for a man with his words to praise his friendly lord,   3175
share the love from his heart, when the lord must go,

---

*As appropriate for mourning.

passing beyond the bounds of his body.
Thus the people of the Geats gave way to grief,
the king's hearth-companions mourning his fall.
They said that he was, among all the world's kings, 3180
the mildest of men, and the most kind in giving,
the most gentle of men, and the most eager for fame.

Endnotes

1. (p. 3, line 1) *Spear-Danes:* This is one of the epithets for the Danes. Others include Scyldings (line 30; after Scyld, the legendary founder of the Danish royal line) and Ring-Danes (line 116). Epithets are common in epics and probably reflect their use in oral tradition. They are frequently attached to the names of prominent figures—for example, Hrothgar is referred to as the "protector of the people" (line 1390) and God as "Ruler of Heaven."

2. (p. 3, line 11) *That was a good king!* This is the first of many instances in which the anonymous poet-narrator inserts a comment into the narrative. Such comments generally point to the value of a person or a person's actions, though some comments apply a Christian religious interpretation to an event that has just occurred. A notable example early in the poem is in lines 175–188, when the poet-narrator reflects on "heathen" religious practices from a Christian point of view.

3. (p. 3, line 18) *Beow:* The manuscript and some modern editions have "Beowulf," but many scholars prefer the form given here to distinguish this Danish king from the hero of the epic.

4. (p. 3, lines 20–25) *The young man did as he ought. . . . shall a man prosper among all the peoples:* This is one of numerous comments the poet-narrator makes on the proper behavior for a ruler and his followers. In his *Germania* (about 98 C.E.), the Roman historian Tacitus refers to a code of behavior between commander and follower as *comitatus.* According to Tacitus, the good ruler gives out gifts, and the followers are bound in loyalty to stand by the ruler in time of need. Such gift-giving is one of the major themes in *Beowulf.*

5. (p. 4, line 35) *in the bosom of the ship:* Funerals involving ship burials or, as described here, sending the dead person out to sea in a ship were apparently common, at least for members of the upper classes, whose ships would be loaded with precious items for this last journey. The greatest discovery of a ship burial in England (from around 650) was at Sutton Hoo, and artifacts from the find are now on view in the British Museum. Note the parallel between Scyld's funeral and that of Beowulf at the end of the epic.

6. (p. 5, line 62) *[. . . was On]ela's queen:* The manuscript is defective here, and the line has been emended by Friedrich Klaeber and other editors. It would appear that Healfdene's daughter was married to Onela, the Swedish king. If this is the case, the marriage would have had a political function—a common theme in this early literature. Such emendations are common in *Beowulf*, as modern editors try to restore letters, words, or even whole lines lost through damage to the manuscript.

7. (p. 5, line 69) *a great mead-hall:* The mead hall, sometimes called a beer hall, was the social and political center for the royal family and their loyal followers. As an institution, therefore, it has great importance throughout the epic.

8. (p. 6, line 85) *would waken their feud after deadly hatred:* This line anticipates enmity that is further described later in the poem (lines 2020–2069): Hrothgar will marry his daughter Freawaru to Ingeld, a prince of the Heathobards, to settle a feud between their two peoples. But the feud will erupt again in bitter conflict between father-in-law and son-in-law, leading to the destruction of Heorot. Women given in such political marriages were often called "peace-weavers" or "peace-pledges," though the peace often did not last.

9. (p. 6, line 90) *song of the scop:* The *scop* (pronounced "shop") was a traditional singer of tales who was trained in both traditional stories and traditional poetic forms. Typically, the scop performed narrative songs orally to the accompaniment of a harp. The poet-narrator of *Beowulf* appears to have been such a scop, or at least to have been thoroughly familiar with the scop's traditional art.

10. (pp. 8–9, lines 175–188) *prayed in heathen temples. . . . may seek the Ruler for peace and protection in the Father's arms:* This passage shows how the poet-narrator and, presumably, the Anglo-Saxon audience saw a distance between themselves and the time before the Christian conversions.

11. (p. 13, lines 303–306) *Images of boars shone . . . watched over life for the grim ones:* Boars were associated with warriors, and like other animal images (such as bears, wolves, ravens, and eagles), they often appear in heroic descriptions in poetry and the visual arts.

12. (p. 18, lines 459–472) *a great feud. . . . and Ecgtheow swore oaths to me:* Hrothgar relates the feud between Beowulf's father Ecgtheow and a people named the Wulfings. Ecgtheow was forced to flee his own land and seek refuge among the Danes. Hrothgar settled the feud by sending treasures to the Wulfings, and this placed Ecgtheow under an obligation to

Hrothgar that Beowulf, as his son, will now honor by coming to the aid of the Danes.

13. (p. 19, line 499) *Unferth:* He is a noble thane in Hrothgar's court who tests Beowulf by questioning his strength as a hero. He now relates an orally circulated legend about a swimming match (some scholars suggest a rowing contest) in the sea between Beowulf and Breca, claiming that Breca proved to have greater strength. Beowulf replies with his own account, which stresses his heroic fights against sea monsters after being separated from Breca in a storm. In this way, Beowulf establishes his credentials to fight Grendel. The exchange is a kind of debate called the *flyting,* and this form was popular throughout the Middle Ages and even later.

14. (p. 32, line 901) *outshining Heremod whose glory grew less:* Immediately after hearing the story of Sigemund, we are given, by negative association, an account of the bad king Heremod.

15. (p. 37, line 1068) *the story of Finn's sons:* This is the beginning of the so-called Finn Episode, which is also related in the Old English poem *The Fight at Finnsburg.* That poem includes some details not given in *Beowulf* but a more comprehensive version (which has not come down to us) must have been known to the audience of both poems. As told in *Beowulf,* a great battle had already taken place between Jutes living in Frisia and a party of Danes. The Danes, led by Hnaef, were visiting the Jutes, whose king, Finn, was married to the Danish Hildeburh. Fighting broke out, and Hnaef, the son of Hildeburh and Finn, and numerous warriors on both sides were killed. After a truce, the Danes were forced by winter weather to stay as guests of the Jutes. The peace was broken, and the Danes under their leader Hengest killed Finn and returned with Hildeburh to their homeland. Once again, we see a woman given in marriage as a "peace-weaver," along with the fragile nature of such an arrangement.

16. (p. 41, line 1203) *on his last expedition:* Hygelac went on a raid in Frisia, where he was killed by a combined force of Franks and Frisians. The raid is also mentioned in independent historical sources, and here in the poem it preoccupies much of Beowulf's thought as he laments the death of his lord. The death of Hygelac is thus important in itself, but it is also the first in a sequence of events that lead to Beowulf becoming king of the Geats.

17. (pp. 64–65, lines 1931–1942) *far different from Modthryth. . . . she should be a peace-weaver:* Though she is a negative example of a queen, introduced as a contrast to Hygd, Modthryth was reformed after her marriage to King Offa, which made her a "peace-weaver."

18. (pp. 66–67, lines 1994–1997) *"For long I entreated you . . . war with Grendel"*: What Hygelac says here is not consistent with the advice Beowulf received from the wise counselors of the Geats before setting off to fight Grendel (lines 202–204). But, of course, Hygelac could have given advice that differed from that of the counselors.

19. (p. 73, line 2188) *not qualified as a war-lord:* This passage provides an example of the common motif of the unpromising youth who goes on to become a hero.

20. (p. 74, lines 2226–2231) *[Then when he saw the monster. . . . stealing]:* The manuscript is damaged at these lines, and the translation here follows the reconstruction by Friedrich Klaeber and other editors. It should be noted, however, that such reconstructions are speculative at best.

21. (p. 75, lines 2247–2266) *"Hold safely. . . . many nations of men!":* This speech, known as the Lay of the Last Survivor, employs the famous motif of *ubi sunt* (Latin for "Where are they now?"), which was common in Old English and other medieval poetry. The motif contrasts the bygone joys of some past time with a lament over their absence in the present.

22. (p. 77, line 2331) *breaking ancient law:* Although the context suggests that the "ancient law" comes from the Christian God, it is possible that it has some connection to the heroic code of the North. In either case, it is not clear what the law may have been.

23. (p. 78, lines 2361–2362) *having captured alone thirty coats of armor . . . the sea-side:* This is yet another of Beowulf's famous swimming feats that emphasize his astounding strength, though some scholars would interpret the action here as rowing over the sea, not swimming. From the passage it is not completely clear whether Beowulf carried the thirty suits of armor on his journey home or, as this translation suggests, stripped armor from thirty foes in battle before setting out.

24. (p. 79, lines 2379–2390) *Ohtere's sons from over the sea. . . . That was a good king:* After Hygelac's death, Heardred becomes king of the Geats, supported by Beowulf. Heardred takes into his protection Eanmund and Eadgils, the two young sons of Ohtere, the Swedish king who has just died. Eanmund and Eadgils have fled Sweden after Onela, their uncle, usurped the Swedish throne and attacked them. (Eanmund was next in line to be king.) Onela then attacks Heardred, who is killed in the fighting, along with Eanmund. With Heardred dead, Beowulf succeeds to the throne as king of the Geats.

25. (p. 79, lines 2391–2396) *vengeance in mind for Heardred's fall.... taking life from King Onela:* Partly to avenge the death of Heardred, and partly to support the cause of the Swedish Eadgils, Beowulf (now king) wages war against the usurper Onela and kills him. Eadgils will now be the rightful heir to be king of the Swedes.

26. (p. 81, lines 2446–2459) *sings a lay for his lament.... happy notes in the hall, as it used to do:* Along with the Lay of the Last Survivor (see note 21), this lay helps to establish the elegiac tone of the last part of the epic, leading to the death of Beowulf and the impending doom for his people.

27. (p. 82, line 2475) *sons of Ongentheow the Swede:* At some time earlier than the events described in note 24, Ohtere and Onela, sons of the Swedish king Ongentheow, attacked the Geats. In the ensuing Battle of Ravenswood, Haethcyn, the king of the Geats, was killed. Hygelac, his brother, succeeded him as king and led a relief force that killed Ongentheow.

28. (p. 87, lines 2611–2616) *the trophies taken from Eanmund, the son of Ohtere.... gifts given him by Onela:* Weohstan was in the service of the usurping Swedish King Onela, who fought against his nephews Eanmund and Eadgils (see note 24).

29. (p. 96, line 2925) *Ravenswood:* This reference begins a long retelling of the Battle of Ravenswood, which took place around the stronghold of Ongentheow, the Swedish king (see note 27). The Geats attacked the Swedes, and Ongentheow killed Haethcyn, king of the Geats. Hygelac, Haethcyn's brother, arrived with a relief force, and Ongentheow was forced to retreat to his stronghold. There he wounded the Geatish warrior Wulf, whose brother Eofer then killed him.

30. (p. 100, lines 3024–3027) *"the dark raven ... both feasted on corpses":* In Old English poetry, the raven, the eagle, and the wolf are traditionally associated with death in battle, evidently because of their propensity to feed on the bodies of fallen warriors.

31. (p. 101, line 3075) *the power of God alone to give treasures:* This passage has puzzled many scholars. In this translation, the interpretation is that a curse was placed on anyone who might disturb the hoard—unless God gave the person leave to do so.

Inspired by Beowulf

J. R. R. Tolkien and The Lord of the Rings

J. R. R. Tolkien, best known as the author of *The Lord of the Rings* trilogy (1954–1955), originated the modern critical view of *Beowulf*. A professor of Anglo-Saxon and English language and literature at the University of Oxford, Tolkien was the first scholar to assert that *Beowulf* was a poem with deep literary value rather than a historical curiosity, a relic of primitive Anglo-Saxon civilization that did not meet the standards of high art. His tract "*Beowulf:* The Monsters and the Critics" (1936) set the stage for modern *Beowulf* criticism, which treats the poem as a sophisticated human accomplishment.

Beowulf served as a foundation text for Tolkien's *The Lord of the Rings*, a novel published in three parts that is among the most powerful fantasy writing of the twentieth century. The award-winning film adaptations directed by Peter Jackson (2001–2003) have further enshrined Tolkien's reputation. *Beowulf* resonates strongly throughout *The Lord of the Rings* and its prequel, *The Hobbit*. The symbolic importance of rings and the use of "middle-earth" as the setting for the novels appear to be drawn from *Beowulf*, and the spirit of the epic influences Tolkien's depictions of larger-than-life heroes, fully developed monster characters, fantastical rural environments, and the bitter struggle between good and evil.

Tolkien was famous for his recitations of *Beowulf* in the original Old English. The poet W. H. Auden attended Tolkien's *Beowulf* classes while at Oxford and later wrote to the author: "I don't think I have ever told you what an unforgettable experience it was to me as an undergraduate, hearing you recite *Beowulf*. The voice was the voice of Gandalf."

Poetry

One of the first important poets to be inspired by *Beowulf* was Alfred, Lord Tennyson (1809–1892), who published a partial translation of the poem in 1830. Henry Wadsworth Longfellow (1807–1882), the most popular nineteenth-century poet in America, followed Tennyson's lead in 1838 and also translated a portion of the poem.

Richard Wilbur, who later became poet laureate of the United States, published his "Beowulf" in *Ceremony and Other Poems* (1950). Casting the landscape as a main character, Wilbur begins: "The land was overmuch like scenery." Wallace Stevens, a giant of American modernism, published his *Beowulf*-influenced poem "The Auroras of Autumn" (1950) in a volume of the same title. Stevens opens on a haunting, sinister note: "This is where the serpent lives, the bodiless." British poet W. H. Auden's tribute to J. R. R. Tolkien, "Short Ode to a Philologist" (1962), also shows the influence of *Beowulf*. Argentine writer Jorge Luis Borges wrote several works in Spanish that reflect his interest in the epic, including an essay on *Beowulf* in 1951. A 1961 Borges poem appeared in *Poetry* magazine in 1993 as "Poem Written in a Copy of *Beowulf*." In this verse, Borges seems to lament years of his life lost to studying the impenetrable "language of the blunt-tongued Anglo-Saxons," which he eventually forgets anyway.

Fiction and Fantasy

The *Beowulf* story has also proved to be fruitful source material for fiction and fantasy writing. W. H. Canaway made use of the poem in his historical novel *The Ring-Givers* (1958). John Gardner's *Grendel* (1971), a narrative told in the first person by Beowulf's monstrous adversary, is probably the best-loved fictional adaptation of the poem. In Australia, the book was made into an animated musical film, *Grendel, Grendel, Grendel* (1981). Popular science-fiction author Michael Crichton invoked *Beowulf* in *Eaters of the Dead* (1971), a thriller that describes the journey a young Arab man takes with a group of Vikings through Northern Europe in the year 922. The book was later filmed as *The Thirteenth Warrior* (1999), starring Antonio Banderas, and has been reissued under that title.

Noted science-fiction authors Larry Niven, Jerry Pournelle, and Steven Barnes co-wrote *The Legacy of Heorot* (1987), a gory retelling of *Beowulf* set on the planet Tau Ceti Four. Tom Holt's witty novel *Who's Afraid of Beowulf?* (1988) takes characters from several Viking romances and transports them to modern-day Scotland in an amusing slapstick adventure story. The book was later republished as *Expecting Beowulf* (2002). Fantasy writer Parke Godwin published a novelistic retelling of the poem, called *The Tower of Beowulf* (1995), that vividly imagines the history of Grendel and Grendel's mother. Frank Schaefer's *Whose Song Is Sung* (1996) tells the story of Beowulf through the eyes of Musculus, a worldly but jaded dwarf who survives his warrior friend and recounts their times together in tough, compelling prose.

Other Works

Beowulf also inspired works in many other media throughout the twentieth century. In 1925 distinguished American composer Howard Hanson (1896–1981), the son of Swedish immigrants, wrote "Lament for Beowulf," a piece for chorus and orchestra. The rock opera *Beowulf* appeared in 1977, with lyrics by Betty Jane Wylie and music by Victor Davies. In film, a post-apocalyptic, science-fiction *Beowulf* debuted in 1999, starring Christopher Lambert. Comic books inspired by the poem include *Beowulf: The Dragon Slayer* (1975–1996), by Michael Uslan, and *Beowulf, Adapted from the 8th Century Epic Poem* (1984), by Jerry Bingham. Matt Wagner's *Grendel*—a mainstay in the underground comics arena since it was first published in the 1980s—darkly chronicles a number of worlds in which Grendel-like monsters abound. Finally, the book *Beowulf: A Likeness* (1990), a collaboration between a poet, a historian, and a designer, features photographs of Germanic archeological sites and artifacts alongside interpretive commentary, and a translation that adds new scenes and backgrounds to the poem.

Comments & Questions

This section provides responses to Beowulf *from early readers of the poem, which began to appear shortly after the work became generally available in the original and in translation during the nineteenth century. They are presented here because they first established the importance of the poem, and thus they are largely responsible for its continuing importance in the curriculum as a "classic." This section then concludes with passages from J. R. R. Tolkien's "Beowulf:* The Monsters and the Critics" (1936), which refocused our attention on the poem as a great work of art and became the foundational text in modern criticism. Those who want to investigate modern views since Tolkien in greater detail will find numerous references in the Introduction to this edition and in the section entitled* For Further Reading. *Following the Comments is a series of Questions drawing attention to various aspects of the poem and inviting readers to explore some of the many complexities of this enduring work.*

Comments

JOHN JOSIAS CONYBEARE

This singular production [Beowulf], independently of its value as ranking among the most perfect specimens of the language and versification of our ancestors, offers an interest exclusively its own. It is unquestionably the earliest composition of the heroic kind extant in any language of modern, or rather of barbarous, Europe.

—from *Illustrations of Anglo-Saxon Poetry* (1826)

THOMAS WRIGHT

The poem of *Beowulf* is a magnificent and accurate picture of life in the heroic ages. Its plot is simple; a few striking instances, grandly traced, and casting strong and broad shadows, form the picture. It is a story of open, single-handed warfare, where love is never introduced as a motive of action, or stratagem as an instrument. Beowulf, like Hercules, seeks glory only by clearing the world of monsters and oppressors.

—from *Fraser's Magazine* (July 1835)

HENRY WADSWORTH LONGFELLOW

One of the oldest and most important remains of Anglo-Saxon literature is the epic poem of Beowulf. Its age is unknown; but it comes from a very distant and hoar antiquity; somewhere between the seventh and tenth centuries. It is like a piece of ancient armour; rusty and battered, and yet strong. From within comes a voice sepulchral, as if the ancient armour spoke, telling a simple, straightforward narrative; with here and there the boastful speech of a rough, old Dane, reminding one of those made by the heroes of Homer. The style, likewise is simple,—perhaps we should say, austere. The bold metaphors, which characterize nearly all the Anglo-Saxon poems we have read, are for the most part wanting in this. The author seems mainly bent upon telling us how his Sea-Goth slew the Grendel and the Fire-drake.

—from the *North American Review* (1838)

ISAAC DISRAELI

Beowulf, a chieftain of the Western Danes, was the Achilles of the North. . . . We first view him with his followers landing on the shores of a Danish kingling. A single ship with an armed company, in those predatory days, could alarm a whole realm. The petty independent provinces of Greece afford a parallel; for Thucydides has marked this period in society, when plunder well fought for was honoured as an heroic enterprise. When a vessel touched on a strange shore, the adventurers were questioned 'whether they were thieves?' a designation which the inquirers did not intend as a term of reproach, nor was it scorned by the valiant; for the spoliation of foreigners at a time when the law of nations had no existence, seemed no disgrace, while it carried with it something of glory, when the chieftain's sword maintained the swarm of his followers, or acquired for himself an extended dominion. . . .

The exploits of Beowulf are of a supernatural cast; and the circumstance has bewildered his translator amid mythic allusions, and thus the hero sinks into the incarnation of a Saxon idol,—a protector of the human race. It is difficult to decide whether the marvellous incidents be mythical, or merely exaggerations of the northern poetic faculty. We, however, learn by these, that corporeal energies and an indomitable spirit were the glories of the hero-life; and the outbreaks of their self-complacency resulted from their own convictions, after many a fierce trial.

—from *Amenities of Literature,*
Consisting of Sketches and Characters of English Literature (1841)

JOHN RICHARD GREEN

It is not indeed in Woden-worship or in the worship of the older gods of flood and fell that we must look for the real religion of our fathers. The song of Beowulf, though the earliest of English poems, is as we have it now a poem of the eighth century, the work it may be of some English missionary of the days of Bæda and Boniface who gathered in the very homeland of his race the legends of its earlier prime. But the thin veil of Christianity which he has flung over it fades away as we follow the hero-legend of our fathers; and the secret of their moral temper, of their conception of life breathes through every line. Life was built with them not on the hope of a hereafter, but on the proud self-consciousness of noble souls.

—from *History of the English People* (1877–1880)

WILLIAM JOHN COURTHOPE

It is evident that the style of *Beowulf* is not that of a literary poet, but of a minstrel. Had it been a deliberate literary composition, it would have exhibited some traces of central design, and its joints and articulations would have been carefully marked; but the poem as it stands is a medley of heterogeneous materials, singularly wanting in plan and consistency. A literary 'Demiurgus' of Anglo-Saxon descent, and separated by a long period from the events which he professed to be recording, would undoubtedly have tried to produce an appearance of order in his creation, by furnishing a clue to his historical allusions. But nothing can be more careless and casual than his references to the heroic exploits, the family relationships, and the tribal feuds of the persons and nations mentioned in the course of the story. This is just what might be expected in the style of oral minstrelsy; it is indeed an exact reproduction of the style of Homer.

—from *A History of English Poetry* (1895–1910)

STOPFORD BROOKE

Beowulf is a complete poem. Its age dignifies it, excuses its want of form, and demands our reverence.

What poetic standard it reaches is another question. It has been called an epic, but it is narrative rather than epic poetry. The subject has not the weight or dignity of an epic poem, nor the mighty fates round which an epic should revolve. Its story is rather personal than national. The one epic quality it has, the purification of the hero, the evolution of his character through trial into perfection—and Beowulf passes from the isolated hero into the image of an heroic king who dies for his people—may belong to a narrative poem. . . . There is also a force, vitality, clearness, and distinctiveness of portraiture, not only in Beowulf's personality but in that of the other personages, which raise the poem into a high place, and predict that special excellence of personal portraiture which made the English drama so famous in the world. Great imagination is not one of the excellences of *Beowulf,* but it has pictorial power of a fine kind, and the myth of summer and winter on which it rests is out of the imagination of the natural and early world. It has a clear vision of places and things and persons; it has preserved for us two monstrous types out of the very early world. When we leave out the repetitions which oral poetry created and excuses, it is rapid and direct; and the dialogue is brief, simple and human. Finally, we must not judge it in study. If we wish to feel whether Beowulf is good poetry, we should place ourselves, as evening draws on, in the hall of folk, when the benches are filled with warriors, merchants and seamen, and the Chief sits in the high seat, and the fires flame down the midst, and the cup goes round—and hear the Shaper strike the harp to sing this heroic lay. Then, as he sings of the great fight with Grendel or the dragon, of the treasure-giving of the king, and of the well-known swords, of the sea-rovings and the sea-hunts and the brave death of men, to sailors who knew the storms, to the fierce rovers who fought and died with glee, to great chiefs who led their warriors, and to warriors who never left a shield, we feel how heroic the verse is, how passionate with national feeling, how full of noble pleasure. The poem is great in its own way, and the way is an English way. The men, the women, at home and in war, are one in character with us. It is our Genesis, the book of our origins.

—from *English Literature from the Beginning to the Norman Conquest* (1898)

W. P. KER

One would like to think of the Anglo-Saxon epic, with *Beowulf* its representative (out of a number of lost heroes), as naturally developing to its full proportions from earlier ruder experimental work, through a course of successive improvements like those that can be traced, for instance, in the growth of the Drama or the Novel. And one wishes there were more left to show how it came about, and also that the process had gone a little further. But not only is there a want of specimens for the literary museum; there is the misgiving that this comparatively well-filled narrative poetry may not be an independent product of the English or the Teutonic genius. There is too much education in *Beowulf*, and it may be that the larger kind of heroic poem was attained in England only through the example of Latin narrative. . . .

The great beauty, the real value, of *Beowulf* is in its dignity of style. In construction it is curiously weak, in a sense preposterous; for while the main story is simplicity itself, the merest commonplace of heroic legend, all about it in the historical allusions, there are revelations of a whole world of tragedy, plots different in import from that of Beowulf, more like the tragic themes of Iceland. Yet with this radical defect, a disproportion that puts the irrelevances in the centre and the serious things on the outer edges, the poem of *Beowulf* is unmistakably heroic and weighty. The thing itself is cheap; the moral and the spirit of it can only be matched among the noblest authors. It is not in the operations against Grendel, but in the humanities of the more leisurely interludes, the conversation of Beowulf and Hrothgar, and such things, that the poet truly asserts his power. It has often been pointed out how like the circumstances are in the welcome of Beowulf at Heorot and the reception of Ulysses in Phœacia. Hrothgar and his queen are not less gentle than Alcinous and Arete. There is nothing to compare with them in the Norse poems: it is not till the prose histories of Iceland appear that one meets with the like temper there. It is not common in any age; it is notably wanting in Middle English literature, because it is an aristocratic temper, secure of itself, and not imitable by the poets of an uncourtly language composing for a simple-minded audience.

This dignity of the epic strain is something real, something in the blood, not a mere trick of literary style. It is lost in the revolution of the eleventh century, but it survives at any rate to the days of Ethelred the Unready and the Battle of Maldon.

—from *The Dark Ages* (1904)

J. R. R. TOLKIEN

A Christian was (and is) still like his forefathers a mortal hemmed in a hostile world. The monsters remained the enemies of mankind, the infantry of the old war, and became inevitably the enemies of the one God, *ece Dryhten*, the eternal Captain of the new. Even so, the vision of the war changes. For it begins to dissolve, even as the contest on the fields of Time thus takes on its largest aspect. The tragedy of the great temporal defeat remains for a while poignant, but ceases to be finally important. It is no defeat, for the end of the world is part of the design of Metod, the Arbiter, who is above the mortal world. Beyond there appears a possibility of eternal victory (or eternal defeat), and the real battle is between the soul and its adversaries. . . . But that shift is not complete in *Beowulf*—whatever may have been true of its period in general. Its author is still concerned primarily with *man on earth*, rehandling in a new perspective an ancient theme: that man, each man and all men, and all their works shall die. . . .

The general structure of the poem . . . is not really difficult to perceive, if we look to the main points, the strategy, and neglect the many points of minor tactics. We must dismiss, of course, from mind the notion that *Beowulf* is a 'narrative poem', that it tells a tale or intends to tell a tale sequentially. The poem 'lacks steady advance': so [the great editor] Klaeber heads a critical section in his edition. But the poem was not meant to advance, steadily or unsteadily. It is essentially a balance, an opposition of ends and beginnings. In its simplest terms, it is a contrasted description of two moments in a great life, rising and setting; an elaboration of the ancient and intensely moving contrast between youth and age, first achievement and final death. It is divided in consequence into two opposed portions, different in matter, manner, and length: A from 1 to 2199 (including an exordium of 52 lines); B from 2200 to 3182 (the end). There is no reason to cavil at this proportion; in any case, for the purpose and the production of the required effect, it proves in practice to be right.

—from "Beowulf: The Monsters and the Critics,"
in *Proceedings of the British Academy* (1936)

Questions

1. Can you identify elements in the poem that hearken back to an ancient time before the coming of Christianity to the peoples of Northern Europe? Do the scattered passages of Christian piety in *Beowulf* seem to you to be an intrusive overlay, or do they feel like an integral and consistent part of the whole?

2. What are Beowulf's strengths as a leader in the expedition to cleanse Hrothgar's hall? What are his strengths as king in the latter part of the poem? Does he also exhibit weaknesses in either of these stages of his life?

3. What is the importance of gift-giving in the poem? Does it appear to emphasize the value of sharing wealth to promote mutual loyalty, rather than hoarding treasure for oneself?

4. What is the role of women in the poem? Are there significantly different codes of behavior for women and men?

5. Do Grendel and Grendel's mother strike you as symbolic—not just as ferocious monsters—but as standing for something more dangerous, if less tangible? If so, what? How about the dragon?

6. Given the many narratives, or pieces of narratives, inserted in the main story line throughout the poem, do you think that *Beowulf* is nevertheless in some sense unified? Why, or why not?

7. What point is being made by the fact that even Beowulf, this great hero, has to die?

8. The poet-narrator makes constant references to stories that have been widely *told* and that he has *heard* from others. What do these references tell us about social interactions in the culture of *Beowulf*? Do they enhance the credibility of his accounts? Do they detract from the originality of the poem as a work of art?

For Further Reading

Editions of Beowulf

Jack, George, ed. *Beowulf: A Student Edition.* Oxford: Oxford University Press, 1994. With marginal glosses of Old English words and fine notes, this is a good choice for the beginning reader who wants to tackle the poem in the original.

Klaeber, Friedrich, ed. *Beowulf and the Fight at Finnsburg.* Third edition. Boston: D. C. Heath, 1950. The standard scholarly edition of the poem.

Mitchell, Bruce, and Fred C. Robinson, eds. *Beowulf: An Edition.* Oxford: Blackwell, 1998. An excellent edition, with much background information.

Surveys of Scholarship and Criticism

Bjork, Robert E., and John D. Niles, eds. *A Beowulf Handbook.* Lincoln: University of Nebraska Press, 1997. Eighteen specialists present clear and well-informed critical surveys of the major topics in *Beowulf* scholarship and criticism over the last two centuries.

Orchard, Andy. *A Critical Companion to Beowulf.* Rochester, NY: D. S. Brewer, 2003. A learned introduction to the scholarship on the poem that provides very wide coverage.

Cultural Context

Canadé Sautman, Francesca, Diane Conchado, and Giuseppe DiScipio, eds. *Telling Tales: Medieval Narratives and the Folk Tradition.* New York: St. Martin's Press, 1998. A wide range of studies of the forms of medieval storytelling.

Foley, John Miles. *The Singer of Tales in Performance.* Bloomington: Indiana University Press, 1995. A clear presentation of oral composition by a leading scholar.

Garmonsway, G. N., and Jacqueline Simpson, eds. *Beowulf and Its Analogues.* Translated by Garmonsway and Simpson; with an essay, "Archaeology and *Beowulf*," by Hilda Ellis Davidson.

London: J. M. Dent, 1968. Especially useful for its translations of a large number of early medieval works that many scholars believe are analogous to *Beowulf*, including an eyewitness account of a Viking funeral by Arabic traveler Ibn Fadlan.

Godden, Malcolm, and Michael Lapidge, eds. *The Cambridge Companion to Old English Literature.* Cambridge: Cambridge University Press, 1991. Essays by various scholars introduce students to the wide variety of literature from the period.

Greenfield, Stanley B., and Daniel G. Calder. *A New Critical History of Old English Literature.* With "A Survey of the Anglo-Latin Background," by Michael Lapidge. New York: New York University Press, 1986. An eminently readable overview of the literature of the Anglo-Saxons.

Lindahl, Carl, John McNamara, and John Lindow, eds. *Medieval Folklore: An Encyclopedia of Myths, Legends, Tales, Beliefs, and Customs.* 2 vols. Santa Barbara, CA: ABC–CLIO, 2000. A standard reference work on the folklore and folklife of various medieval cultures, with more than 300 articles by specialists, including articles on *Beowulf* and the Anglo-Saxon period in English history, together with many more on specific topics relating to the poem.

Lord, Albert B. *The Singer of Tales.* Cambridge, MA: Harvard University Press, 1960. Indispensable for the study of oral composition; by one of the founders of the field.

Mitchell, Bruce. *An Invitation to Old English and Anglo-Saxon England.* Oxford: Blackwell, 1995. A book for students, introducing the fundamentals of the language in the context of the culture of the Anglo-Saxons.

Outlaws and Other Medieval Heroes. Southern Folklore 53 (1996; special issue). Interesting views from a folkloric perspective, including two on *Beowulf.*

A Selection of Studies of the Poem

Baker, Peter S., ed. *The Beowulf Reader.* New York: Garland Publishing, 2000.

Fulk, R. D., ed. *Interpretations of Beowulf: A Critical Anthology.* Bloomington: Indiana University Press, 1991.

Hill, John M. *The Cultural World of Beowulf.* Toronto: University of Toronto Press, 1995.

Irving, Edward B. *A Reading of Beowulf.* New Haven, CT: Yale University Press, 1968.

———. *Rereading Beowulf.* Philadelphia: University of Pennsylvania Press, 1989.

Kiernan, Kevin. *Beowulf and the Beowulf Manuscript.* Revised edition, with a foreword by Katherine O'Brien O'Keefe. Ann Arbor: University of Michigan Press, 1996.

Newton, Sam. *The Origins of Beowulf and the Pre-Viking Kingdom of East Anglia.* Rochester, NY: D. S. Brewer, 1993.

Niles, John D. *Beowulf: The Poem and Its Tradition.* Cambridge, MA: Harvard University Press, 1983.

———. *Homo Narrans: The Poetics and Anthropology of Oral Literature.* Philadelphia: University of Pennsylvania Press, 1999.

O'Keefe, Katherine O'Brien. *Visible Song: Transitional Literacy in Old English Verse.* Cambridge: Cambridge University Press, 1990.

Overing, Gillian R. *Language, Sign, and Gender in Beowulf.* Carbondale: Southern Illinois University Press, 1990.

Robinson, Fred C. *Beowulf and the Appositive Style.* Knoxville: University of Tennessee Press, 1985.

Tolkien, J. R. R. "*Beowulf*: The Monsters and the Critics." *Proceedings of the British Academy* 22 (1936), pp. 245–295. Reprinted in Fulk's *Interpretations of Beowulf* (see above).

Online Resources

The Labyrinth: Resources for Medieval Studies. While many Web sites are unreliable sources of information, this one is excellent. Hosted by Georgetown University, the site contains a treasure hoard of materials relating to *Beowulf* and other works of the Middle Ages. http://www.georgetown.edu/labyrinth/

Electronic Beowulf. This Web site represents a major editorial project under the direction of Kevin Kiernan at the University of Kentucky that is digitizing the *Beowulf* manuscript held by the British Library. The site contains information about the project, as well as images of the manuscript and a new, searchable edition. http://www.uky.edu/~kiernan/eBeowulf/guide.htm